THE SAGAS OF RAGNAR LODBROK

THE SAGAS OF RAGNAR LODBROK

translated by Ben Waggoner

Troth Publications
2009

The Tale of Ragnar's Sons previously appeared in *Idunna*, nos. 78 and 80.

Published by The Troth
24 Dixwell Avenue, Suite 124
New Haven, Connecticut 06511
http://www.thetroth.org/

ISBN-13: 978-0-578-02138-6

Library of Congress Control Number: 2009927840

Cover emblem: Raven emblem from a coin of Anlaf Guthfrithsson, Norse ruler of York, England, 939-941 AD

Troth logo designed by Kveldulf Gundarsson, drawn by 13 Labs, Chicago, Illinois

Cover design: Ben Waggoner

Typeset in Garamond 14/11/9

for my wife

CONTENTS

Introduction

In 1758, Thomas Percy published *Five Pieces of Runic Poetry*, his translation of selected Old Norse poems. One of the poems was *Krákumál*, "Words of the Raven", the ode supposedly chanted by the legendary warrior-king Ragnarr Loðbrók[1], or Ragnar "Shaggy-Breeches", as he died in a pit of snakes. Percy was not the first English author to notice the *Krákumál*: Ole Worm had published a Latin translation in 1635, and in 1700, Sir William Temple quoted this translation of "that song or epicedium of Regner Ladbrog" in his essay "Of Heroic Virtue", noting that "such an alacrity or pleasure in dying was never expressed in any other writing, nor imagined among any other people."[2] Without quoting *Krákumál* directly, John Dryden expressed its lust for heroic death in the libretto for the "semi-opera" *King Arthur*, set to music by Henry Purcell and first performed in 1691:

> Brave souls, to be renown'd in story,
>> Honour prizing,
>> Death despising,
>> Fame acquiring
>> By expiring,
> Die and reap the fruit of glory.[3]

But it was Percy's translations, along with other translations of Old Norse texts by Maillet and others, that started something of a craze for "Nordic" and "Gothic" atmosphere among early Romantic poets. This enthusiasm was part of a larger surge of interest in the heroic past of the British Isles, fed by works such as Macpherson's Ossianic lays and Percy's *Reliques of English Poetry*. The figure of the bloodthirsty yet noble Viking warrior, yearning for brave death on the battlefield in order to gain Valhalla, entered English literature and imagination—in part because, as English scholars often noted, they themselves were descended from the Vikings, from their kin the Angles and Saxons, and from their descendants the Normans.

Introduction

Robert Southey's "The Race of Odin" (1827) is possibly the best-known poem that paid homage to the *Krákumál,* quoting its refrain directly:

> Dark was the dungeon, damp the ground,
>> Beneath the reach of cheering day,
>> Where Regner dying lay;
> Poisonous adders all around
> On the expiring warrior hung,
> Yet the full stream of verse flow'd from his dauntless tongue:
>> "We fought with swords," the warrior cry'd,
>> "We fought with swords," he said—he died.[4]

Southey had made even more use of Ragnar's legend in his dedicatory poem to Amos Cottle's translation of the *Poetic Edda* (1797):

> A strange and savage faith
> Of mightiest power! it fram'd the unfeeling soul
> Stern to inflict and stubborn to endure,
> That laugh'd in death. When round the poison'd breast
> Of Regner clung the viper brood, and trail'd
> Their coiling length along his festering wounds,
> He, fearless in his faith, the death-song pour'd,
> And lived in his past fame; for sure he hoped
> Amid the Spirits of the mighty dead
> Soon to enjoy the fight. And when his sons
> Avenged their father's fate, and like the wings
> Of some huge eagle spread the severed ribs
> Of Ella, in the shield-roof'd hall they thought
> One day from Ella's skull to quaff the mead,
> Their valour's guerdon.[5]

The joyous acceptance of violent death in order to gain Valhalla's glories is clearly taken from *Krákumál.* So is the drinking of ale from enemies' skulls, which is actually derived from a mistranslated figure of speech in the poem, but which remained a part of the Viking image well into the 19th century[6]—Matthew Arnold, in *Balder Dead* (1855), not only gave a speaking part to "Regner, who swept the northern seas with fleets"[7], but mentioned "gold-rimmed skulls" used for wine-glasses in Valhalla.[8] And the infamous "blood-eagle" rite, as described in the *Tale of Ragnar's Sons,* may also derive from misunderstandings of poetic speech—but it, too, has become a part of the image of the Viking warrior.

The early Romantic craze for "Gothic" lore eventually died down—helped along by Alexander Pope, who skewered Ole Worm in the *Dunciad*—but Ragnar was hardly forgotten. Genealogists traced Queen Victoria's lineage to Ragnar.[9] Novelists referred to Ragnar and his kin, and often re-imagined them almost out of recognition, in books from Charles Kingsley's *Hereward* (1865) to Paul du Chaillu's *Ivar the Viking* (1893) to Ottilie Liljencrantz's *The Ward of King Canute* (1903) and Jack London's *The Star-Rover* (1915). Their stories were adapted and suitably moralized for children by the Society for Promoting Christian Knowledge (!) in *Stories of The Norsemen* (1852), by H. A. Guerber in *Legends of the Middle Ages* (1896), and by Eva March Tappan in *In the Days of Alfred the Great* (1900). Translations of *Krákumál* appeared throughout the 19th century,[10] as did adaptations of the stories of the Battle of Brávellir, Ragnar, and Ragnar's sons[11]. More recently, Hollywood adapted Ragnar's story—very loosely—in the 1958 movie *The Vikings*, in which Ragnar was played by Ernest Borgnine, his sons were renamed Eric and Einar, and the snakepit was replaced with a pit of ravenous wolves. Modern authors of historical fiction and fantasy have drawn on the stories of Ragnar and his sons, including Harry Harrison (*The Hammer and the Cross* and its sequels), Bernard Cornwell (*The Last Kingdom* and its sequels), and Nancy Farmer (*The Sea of Trolls*). Even in works that don't derive from Ragnar's own legend, the archetypal "Viking warrior figure" that he represents has influenced creative minds from Thomas Carlyle to Richard Wagner to J. R. R. Tolkien to several contemporary heavy metal bands.[12] Whatever their historical reality, the tales of Ragnar Lodbrok and his sons are important sources of our popular image of what the Vikings were like.

I have translated the three major Old Norse sources for his life and deeds: the *Saga of Ragnar Lodbrok*, the *Tale of Ragnar's Sons*, and the poem *Krákumál*. I have included a fourth Old Norse text telling about Ragnar's purported ancestors: a sizable fragment of a saga, now called *Sögubrot af nokkurum fornkonungum í Dana- ok Svíaveldi*, "Saga Fragment about Certain Ancient Kings of the Danish and Swedish Realms"—usually shortened to *Sögubrot*. To fill in a gap between the *Sögubrot* and the *Saga*, I have also included my translation of a portion of a 16th-century Latin text written by Arngrímr Jónsson, *Ad catalogum regum Sveciæ annotanda* (*List of Swedish Kings*). This is Jónsson's rendition of a portion of the now-lost *Skjöldunga saga*; the *Sögubrot* is thought to be an excerpt of the same saga, and the *Tale of Ragnar's Sons* draws on it extensively.

The sixth major source for Ragnar's life, which in some respects is very different from the others, is chapter IX of Saxo Grammaticus's *Gesta Danorum* (*History of the Danes*). Written in Latin towards the end of the 12th century, Saxo's *History* was heavily influenced by classical Latin authors, but also drew extensively on Norse sources. Saxo himself acknowledged his great debt to the Icelanders, who "regard it a real pleasure to discover and commemorate the achievements of every nation"; he freely acknowledged that he had "scrutinised their store of historical treasures and composed a considerable part of this present work by copying their narratives".[13] Saxo's account of Ragnar's life seems to preserve certain traditions that are missing or only hinted at in the main Norse texts.[14]

These texts vary somewhat in literary quality. *Krákumál*, while put together skilfully enough, seems at first to fit the stereotype of skaldic poetry as "little more than a rhapsody of rejoicing in carnage, a ringing of changes on the biting sword and the flowing of blood and the feast of the raven and the vulture"[15]. The *Tale of Ragnar's Sons* suffers from uneven pacing compared to the *Saga*, with some episodes told in detail and others skimmed over, while the *Saga* itself has some unexplained plot holes (what sort of relationship *do* Aslaug and Eirek have?) Yet the sagas contain finely told stories with memorable characters: the conniving Ivar Wide-Grasp; his clever and pitiless namesake Ivar the Boneless; the strong, fierce, tragic Aslaug. For their value to folklorists and medieval historians, for their impact on later English literature, and for their value as entertaining tales of derring-do, these stories are well worth reading today.

Sagas

A proud nation with a unique form of self-government—"among them there is no king, but only law"[16]—Iceland changed rapidly in the 13th century. Torn apart by bloody feuds among its leading families, it was absorbed into the kingdom of Norway in 1262, eventually becoming an impoverished backwater. Yet even as their commonwealth was dying, Icelanders were creating a body of prose narratives— the sagas—unlike anything else in medieval literature. The sagas are not the oldest prose writings from Iceland: translations of Latin works, law codes, and brief histories were being written in Iceland as early as the mid-12th century. Nor did the sagas come into existence in a vacuum; influences on the sagas range from chivalric romances, to Greek and Latin classics, to Christian homilies and saints' lives, to historical and pseudo-historical chronicles. Nonetheless, the sagas' unique literary style sets them apart from anything else written in Europe at the time.

Common consensus would group the best-known sagas into several major genres. *Íslendingasögur*, "sagas of Icelanders", deal with the first generations of the founding families of Iceland. *Konungasögur*, "kings' sagas", recount the lives of the kings of the Scandinavian realms. *Fornaldarsögur*, "sagas of old times", deal with legendary events and heroes derived from Germanic history, myth, and folklore. The pagan Norse gods occasionally put in appearances, and giants, trolls, enchanters, monsters, and wise kings with beautiful daughters all play their parts against a backdrop of legendary Scandinavia, or even stranger lands in the farthest north of the world.[17] *Riddarasögur*, the "knightly sagas", include both translations of chivalric tales—of Arthur's knights, Charlemagne, and others—and original Icelandic compositions in imitation of these tales. While *riddarasögur* may contain wizards and monsters and giants as the *fornaldarsögur* do, they are generally set in more southerly realms of Europe, or even farther away, in India or Arabia. *Riddarasögur* draw much more extensively on continental ideals of chivalry, praising courtly ideals of behavior and feeling (summed up as *kurteisi*, a word borrowed into Norse from the Old French *corteisie*) and courtly pastimes such as chess and jousting. Finally, there are *samtíðarsögur*, "contemporary sagas", written soon after the events they describe in 13th-century Iceland; *biskupasögur*, "bishops' sagas", about the early bishops of Iceland; *heilagra manna sögur*, "holy men's sagas" or saints' lives; and translations and adaptations of historical and pseudohistorical works about the Trojan War, Roman Republic, and the like.

Legendary sagas and chivalric sagas were quite popular among medieval Icelanders themselves—in fact, such sagas continued to be written, and read, in Iceland up to the early twentieth century.[18] When saga-literature was first discovered by scholars outside of Iceland, the *fornaldarsögur* attracted much attention; they seemed to prove that the Scandinavian kingdoms had a long and glorious past that was every bit as noble and worthy as the heritage of ancient Greece and Rome.[19] More recent tastes give pride of place to the *Íslendingasögur*, which include some undisputed classics: *Njáls saga*, *Laxdæla saga*, and *Egils saga*, for example, are considered among the best prose literary works of the European Middle Ages, as well as sources of social and anthropological information on Icelandic society. The *fornaldarsögur* have not been rated as highly: most are no longer considered to contain much solid historical information, and the best known are often read primarily for their insights into better-known works (*Hrólfs saga kráka* for its links with *Beowulf*, or *Völsunga saga* for its links with the *Nibelunglied*, Wagner's *Ring*, Tolkien's *Lord of the Rings*, and so on). *Riddarasögur* have long been considered almost beneath contempt; few have been translated into English, and scholars have described them as "derivative", "escapist", "dreary", and even "pernicious". It has often been assumed, incorrectly, that the more romantic *fornaldarsögur* and the *riddarasögur* were written long after the loss of Icelandic independence and the high tide of saga writing, as an escapist literature that allowed Icelanders to hide from gloomy reality in a glorious Neverland, even as they introduced foreign styles and themes that degraded the "purity" of the native saga tradition.

The problem with this neat taxonomy is that a great many sagas—quite possibly all of them—incorporate elements of more than one class. The *fornaldarsögur* overlap considerably with the *riddarasögur*, so much so that some prefer to treat them together as one genre, "romances"[20]. Many *fornaldarsögur* contain knightly ideals of kurteisi, exotic settings, and courtly color such as jousting tournaments and heraldic blazons. To give just one example, *Völsunga saga* is often considered the foremost *fornaldarsaga*, containing as it does a heroic legend that was known throughout the Germanic world; yet its hero Sigurd is described in terms that come directly from the *riddarasögur*, with his heraldically emblazoned shield, his wise horse, and his surpassing *kurteisi*.[21] *Konungasögur* that deal with legendary kings, notably *Ynglinga saga*, cover the same ground as certain *fornaldarsögur*. At the same time, some of the tales that are classified as *fornaldarsögur* are not set in the legendary never-never, but in the days of historically attested kings, usually dealing with retainers of theirs who travel to far-off places—such as *Þorsteins þáttr bæjarmagns*, *Helga þáttr Þórissonar*, *Völsa þáttr*, and the ending of *Sörla þáttr*. Other episodes no less "fantastic" than any *fornaldarsögur* are embedded in ostensibly historical kings' sagas; an example would be Odin's visit to Olaf Tryggvason in *Heimskringla*.[22]

Some *Íslendingasögur* digress into fantastic episodes more typical of a *fornaldarsaga*, with much the same kind of lore about trolls and giants that the *fornaldarsögur* present. These include *Gull-Þóris saga*, with its battle against undead Vikings on an Arctic island; *Bjarnar saga hítdælakappa*, whose hero slays a dragon; *Kormaks saga*, whose hero is killed fighting a giant in Scotland; or *Barðs saga snæfellsáss*, with its giants and half-giants living in Iceland's interior wastelands. The completely fantastic *Jökuls þáttr Búasonar* would count as a perfect *fornaldarsaga* if it weren't for the fact that it's written as a sequel to an *Íslendingasaga*, *Kjalnesinga saga*. Another *Íslendingasaga*, *Stjörnu-Odda draumr*, is a romantic *fornaldarsaga* presented as an Icelander's dream. Even the masterpieces among the *Íslendingasögur* include episodes that wouldn't be out of place in a *fornaldarsaga*: the "Lay of the Spear" vision in *Njáls saga*, or the hero's battles with the undead in *Grettis saga*. Other *Íslendingasögur*, such as *Víglunds saga*, show considerable influence from courtly romance; in fact, some of the greatest of the *Íslendingasögur* draw on translated romances such as *Alexanders saga*.[23] The plot of *Laxdæla saga* seems to have been strongly influenced by the Sigurd cycle, with the Kjartan-Bolli-Gudrun triangle parallelling the Sigurd-Gunnar-Brynhild triangle, and with the noble captive Melkorka playing a similar narrative role to Aslaug in *Ragnars saga*.[24]

The sagas in this book clearly illustrate the problems of saga classification. They are all usually considered *fornaldarsögur*, and all have many elements of this type. But the *Sögubrot* is thought to be a fragment of *Skjöldunga saga*, which is considered a "king's saga". Although the *Sögubrot* is considered to be close to the *fornaldarsögur* in style and subject matter, it is relatively free of the stock elements of a *fornaldarsaga*; there are no trolls or giants, no deities appear in person, and the most fantastic elements are Hraerek's and Ivar's prophetic dreams, which resemble dream episodes in sagas of all types. At the same time, its jousting scene in Chapter 2, using the borrowed word *turniment*, is a touch from the *riddarasögur*. The *Þáttr af Ragnars sonum* begins like a *fornaldarsaga*, but it ends with historically attested kings, and in fact its final section is almost identical with the last chapter of the king's saga *Hálfdanar saga svarta* in *Heimskringla*. And finally, both *Ragnars saga* and the *Þáttr* contain episodes that seem to have been shaped by social concerns in 13th-century Iceland.[25]

In most bookstores today, "serious" literature, science fiction and fantasy, Westerns, horror, and romance will each be found in its own section of shelving. But the writers of sagas didn't think in terms of modern genres; they wanted to create narratives that would entertain, instruct, and sometimes comment on events of the writer's own time. To do this, they were able to pick and choose among various materials at hand to create the most complete or most pleasing narrative. Several scholars have recently argued that the sagas constitute a single genre, not several. It is probably best to think of saga "genres" as types of stylistic elements and source materials, which might be blended in almost any combination. One type might predominate in any given saga, but few if any sagas can truly be said to be "pure".[26]

Sagas were usually assembled from a variety of older sources, both oral and written: the word commonly used to describe saga composition is *samansetja*, "to set together; to assemble". The process was open-ended; later copyists of a saga might add new material, and were sometimes explicitly invited to do so. *Yngvars saga víðförla* gives some insight into how the process of saga composition was done. This saga is known to have been based on a real event, Yngvar's expedition from Sweden deep into Asia in the year 1041. A set of over twenty runestones in Sweden commemorates men who "fell in the East with Yngvar." In the last chapter, the saga's unknown author tells how the saga was assembled:

> We have heard and written this saga according to the direction of the books that the monk Odd the Wise has had made from the accounts of wiser men, as he has said himself in his letter, which he sent to Jon Loptsson and Gizur Hallsson. But they who think that they know more precisely should add to it what now seems to be lacking. Brother Odd says that he had heard the priest named Isleif tell this saga, and also Glum Thorgeirsson, and a third man named Thorir. From their accounts he has included what seemed to him to be the most remarkable. But Isleif is said to have heard Yngvar's story from a merchant, who said that he got it from the retainers of the king of Sweden. Glum got it from his father, and Thorir got it from Klakka Samsson, and Klakka had first heard it from his kin.[27]

Odd the monk had composed the story by assembling the most remarkable elements of the three accounts that he has heard—each of which has passed through at least one or two oral transmissions. The unknown saga author may well have altered the story from Brother Odd's work. More to the point, the author invites later readers to add anything that may be lacking: this saga is not a closed work, but is open to further editing from future generations of readers and hearers. Thus *Yngvars saga*, with a known historical basis, includes realistic, plausible scenes, interspersed with encounters with the giants, dragons, and princesses of many a *fornaldarsaga*, set in a distant, exotic, southern location like those of many a *riddarasaga*.

This approach to saga composition explains the almost kaleidoscopic nature of the sagas of Ragnar. It explains why the *Saga of Ragnar Lodbrok* and *Tale of Ragnar's Sons* include an episode that's borrowed from Geoffroy of Monmouth's *History of the Kings of Britain* (or possibly from the *Aeneid*), several motifs from the Völsung legend, at least two that ultimately derive from the Bible, another from a medieval saint's life, yet another that may be borrowed from Celtic myth, and still others that are widespread motifs in folktales from Ireland to India. It explains how *Hálfs saga ok Hálfsrekka*, which is otherwise unrelated to the Ragnar story, quotes a stanza of the poem that ends the *Saga*, placing it in a completely different context. It explains how Saxo Grammaticus and the *Saga* include some of the same episodes arranged in a different order, such as the death of Hvitserk. It further explains how Sigurd the Volsung, who would have lived in the 5th century (insofar as he can be dated at all), could have a daughter who would marry Ragnar Lodbrok in the 9th century.

That being said, the saga compilers were not uncritical compilers of random anecdotes. In the chapter of *Yngvars saga* quoted above, the author discusses and dismisses alternate stories about the hero: he refutes the suggestion that Yngvar was the son of Eymund Olafsson, and he disagrees with a story that Yngvar sailed down a river whose banks were so high and steep that he had to use candles to navigate in the darkness. Other sagas acknowledge conflicting sources by including alternate versions of a story, with the reader left to decide which is more likely. Chapter 31 of *Göngu-Hrólfs saga*, for example, describes a hero's fate thus: "Books strongly disagree about this matter, because it's said in *Sturlaugs saga* and many other sagas that he died of an illness at home in Ringerike and was buried there in a mound, but here it is said that after Thord fell, Grim Ægir came up out of the earth behind Sturlaug's back and struck with a sword at his spine, so that he was cut in two in the middle. We don't know which is more truthful."[28] The prologue to the same saga notes that "Men are all misinformed in different ways, because frequently what one person sees and hears, another doesn't, though they both happen to be at the event."[29] Still other writers defended their inclusion of improbable-sounding episodes with appeals to ancient authorities; *Vilhjálms saga sjóðs* was allegedly carved on a stone wall in Babylon and written down by Homer, while other sagas make less extravagant claims on the authority of "wise men of old". In all of these ways, the creators of even the most fantastic sagas critically assembled their source material, and grounded their narratives in the real world.

Perhaps the most important way in which sagas were grounded in the real world was through genealogy. Icelanders did not experience most sagas as "pure fantasy" unconnected with their lives, the way that a modern viewer of, say, *Star Wars* would. The great figures of the sagas are all situated within a web of family relationships that extended down to the hearers themselves; the continuity between past and present is fundamental to the mindset of the sagas' compilers and hearers. Many sagas in all genres begin one or a few generations before the protagonists appear, and end with a listing of the descendants of the protagonists, with lines like "and a great family is descended from him". We can see the use of genealogy in an often-quoted extract from chapter 10 of *Þorgils saga ok Haflíða*, one of several sagas that makes up the large *Sturlunga saga*, describing the entertainment at a wedding feast that took place in the year 1119:

> Hrolf of Skalmarnes told a saga about Hrongvid the Viking, and about Olaf King of Warriors, and the breaking into Thrain's burial mound, and Hromund Gripsson, and many verses along with it. King Sverri was amused by this saga, and he called such "lying sagas" the most entertaining. And yet men are able to reckon their ancestry from Hromund Gripsson. Hrolf himself had put this saga together.[30]

A version of this story, although not exactly what Hrolf would have told, is still extant[31], with the same fantastic villains and escapades that are alluded to here—and it mentions that the protagonist Hromund Gripsson had kings and heroes as descendants. *Landnámabók* adds that the first two permanent settlers of Iceland, the cousins Ingolf and Hjorleif, were great-grandsons of Hromund Gripsson; it then lists five generations of Ingolf's descendants, including prominent chieftains and lawspeakers[32]. Readers and hearers of Hromund Gripsson's saga would have known themselves to be descendants of the main characters, or at least would have been familiar with their descendants. Despite King Sverri's apparent skepticism, these genealogical claims anchored the story in the web of familial relationships that permeated Icelandic society, not just in its literature, but in its laws and social organization.[33] If, through some strange quirk of time travel, *Star Wars* had been made by medieval Icelanders, it would have ended by tracing the descendants of Han Solo and Princess Leia down through several generations to an Icelandic family of prosperous farmers and chieftains, well known to the film's viewers.

Ragnars saga mentions that a distinguished lineage of Icelanders was descended from Ragnar, through his son Bjorn Ironside. *Landnámabók* mentions this lineage, descended from Bjorn's great-grandson Hofda-Thord[34]; it also mentions another prominent Icelandic family descended from Ragnar through his daughter Alof[35]. Leading Icelandic families in the twelfth and thirteenth centuries could claim descent from Ragnar and his wife Aslaug—and thus descent, through her, from the most famous of all Germanic heroes, Sigurd the Volsung. The powerful 13th-century Icelandic family of the Oddaverjar (Men of Oddi), which included Snorri Sturluson himself, could claim descent from both the Skjoldung dynasty of Denmark and from Ragnar Lodbrok—and members and associates of the Oddaverjar took a special interest in writing and preserving works concerned with these lineages.[36] Such connections bolstered families' prestige, and they provided descendants with models for heroic behavior. More generally, they provided Icelanders with national pride and consciousness of a shared national history: as the *Melabók* manuscript of the *Landnámabók* puts it, "But we can better answer the criticism of foreigners when they accuse us of coming from slaves or rogues, if we know for certain the truth about our ancestry."[37]

So how to read these sagas? In his famous essay *"Beowulf, The Monsters and the Critics"*, J. R. R. Tolkien gently chastises critics who are disappointed in *Beowulf* "at the discovery that it was itself and not something that the scholar would have liked better—for example, a heathen heroic lay, a history of Sweden, a manual of Germanic antiquities, or a Nordic *Summa Theologica*."[38] The texts presented here may not rival *Beowulf* in literary quality—but like *Beowulf*, they cannot and should not be read as historical documents, anthropological evidence for ancient societies, or heroic heathen tales handed down from purely pagan times. They do contain information that may be useful to historians, anthropologists, and scholars of mythology—but in the end, they stand, or they fall, as stories. They once entertained, instructed, and amused their hearers, and perhaps they can do the same now. More importantly, they situated their hearers' own lives within a network of relationships extending back toward the dim beginning of all things. The audience would have felt "that sense of perspective, of antiquity with a greater and yet darker antiquity behind."[39]

Brávellir

The *Sögubrot* tells of the Battle of Brávellir, an immense battle between the forces of Harald Wartooth and his nephew Hring. *Ynglinga saga*, in Snorri Sturluson's *Heimskringla*, doesn't mention it, even though it covers the time period in which the battle allegedly took place and mentions some relatives of the participants. But other sources emphasize the colossal scale of the battle; *Hervarar saga* calls it one of "the most renowned in the ancient tales, with the greatest count of slain."[40] *Bósa saga ok Herrauðs* states that no fewer than one hundred and sixteen kings were killed in the battle.[41] Saxo claims that 12,000 of Hring's nobles and 30,000 of Harald's nobles were slain—not counting the commoners who died.[42]

The Battle of Brávellir might well have some historical basis, but it is difficult, perhaps impossible, to trace now. A text now called *Ágrip af Sögu Danakonunga* (*Synopsis of a Saga of the Danish Kings*) claims that Sigurd Hring lived during the imperial reign of Charlemagne (800-814).[43] The *Royal Frankish Annals* for the year 812 mention a battle between Sigifrid and Anulo, two rival kings of Denmark, in which 10,940 men are said to have died. Both rivals were killed, but Anulo's forces won, and his brothers Heriold and Reginfrid became joint kings. Anulo is also said to be the nephew of another Heriold.[44] If the name *Anulo* is interpreted as a Latinization of the name *Hringr* ("ring"), then the King Hring of the *Sögubrot*, also known as Sigurd Hring, could be a conflation of Sigifrid and Anulo. Saxo seems to have assumed that Reginfrid was the same as Ragnar Lodbrok, although the Frankish annals state that Reginfrid was killed in 814, which creates chronological difficulties.[45] On the other hand, Saxo places several generations of Danish kings between the Battle of Brávellir and the birth of Ragnar Lodbrok; the Hring of Brávellir and the Hring who is Ragnar's father are not the same person. If Saxo is closer to the truth, then the battle, if it happened at all, could well have taken place a century earlier.

Whatever its historical basis, the Battle of Brávellir draws heavily on myth. Saxo depicts the battle of Brávellir as apocalyptic chaos that reverses the order of creation, in words that sound much like Ragnarök:

> The trumpets blared and each side joined battle with utmost violence. You might well have imagined that the heavens were suddenly rushing down at the earth, woods and fields subsiding, that the whole of creation was in turmoil and had returned to ancient chaos, all things human and divine convulsed by a raging tempest and everything tumbling simultaneously into destruction. When it came to the hurling of spears, the intolerable hiss of the weapons filled the entire air with a din quite unbelievable. The steam from men's wounds drew an unexpected mist across the sky and the daylight was concealed under a hailstorm of missiles.[46]

The belief in a cosmic Last Battle at the end of time, or at the end of a great cycle of time, goes back to Proto-Indo-European roots. However, only in Germanic myths (the myth of Ragnarök) and Persian religion is the Last Battle said to be in the future, fought between the gods and their foes on a cosmic scale. In many Indo-European cultures, the Last Battle has been transferred from the mythic future to the mythical or legendary past—for example, the Irish legend of the Second Battle of Moytura between the Tuatha de Danaan and the Fomoire, or the war between the Olympians and the Titans in Greek mythology. In still others, the Last Battle has become a historical event, like the Roman history of the Battle of Lake Regillus, or the Kurukshetra War in the *Mahabhárata*.[47]

Stig Wikander noted many specific parallels between Saxo's account of Brávellir and the Kurukshetra War in the *Mahabhárata*, and Dumézil has expanded on them. Both have a blind king of a vast empire, the son of a princess and a commoner (Dhrtarastra/Harald) who fights against his nephew/s (the Pandavas/Hring); a mighty warrior wielding a club (Bhima/Bruni); a great warrior born with extra appendages, who commits crimes (Sisupala/Starkad); and another great warrior who fights for the blind king and who is killed by being shot full of arrows (Bhisma/Ubbi).[48] On the third day of the battle, Bhisma leads a formation with a "snout" or "beak" against an opposing crescent-shaped line, just as Ubbi leads the "boar's head" wedge against Hring's crescent-shaped line.[49] Even the imagery is similar: compare the above passage from Saxo with this passage from the *Mahabhárata*, describing the beginning of the Kurukshetra War:

> Then all of a sudden as the mighty Drona gave the command the earth lurched with a terrifying and tortured groan and the tumultuous sky and the sun within it were obscured as a hot storm of dust blew upward like a great curtain of silk, and from the cloudless heavens there poured a rain of gore, bones and blood, and flocks of vultures, hawks, cranes, herons and crows wheeled dizzily above the heads of your soldiers, my king, and with eerie, pitiless howls jackals drew deadly circles around us, hungry and thirsty for flesh and blood. . . . Many and dire were the portents we witnessed. All heralded the massacre of heroes in the battle to come. . . . The whole world filled with the sounds of the armies of the Pándavas and the Káuravas. They crashed together in fury beneath arrows loosed to satisfy the hunger of each to destroy the other.[50]

The problem, as Magnus Wistrand pointed out, is that many of these parallels exist in Saxo's account but are not found in the *Sögubrot*. To give a few examples, in the *Sögubrot* Harald isn't blind, Harald's father isn't a commoner, and Hring's army doesn't defend against the wedge formation with a crescent formation. The generations of dynastic struggles that lead to the battle are comparable between the *Mahabhárata* and Saxo's account, but Harald's ancestry is completely different in the *Sögubrot*.[51] Other similarities between the Brávellir accounts and the *Mahabhárata*, such as the long lists of the armies and champions on each side, the description of battles as a series of single combats, and the birds and canines scavenging the slain corpses, may simply be common Indo-European tropes—they can also be found in the *Iliad*, for example. Nonetheless, even if direct comparisons with the *Mahabhárata* are specious, the Battle of Brávellir may be another instance of the mythic Last Battle reinterpreted as a historical event. If so, Norse lore would have a pair of Last Battles: Ragnarök, set in the mythic future; and the Battle of Brávellir, the same myth turned into legendary history.

Divine Heroes

Harald Wartooth is one of the most "Odinic" heroes anywhere in the Norse lore. Saxo preserves a tradition that Harald's parents were only able to conceive him by visiting the temple at Uppsala and receiving advice from Odin (which is more than a little reminiscent of the story in *Völsunga saga* of how Odin helped with Völsung's conception[52]). Saxo also tells[53] how Odin personally taught Harald to form his army in the wedge formation, called the *svinfylking* or "swine-formation" because it looks like a pig's head from above—and Odin was said to have taught the wedge formation to other favorites of his, notably Hadding[54] and Sigurd the Völsung[55]. Saxo also attributes to Odin's blessing the fact that Harald cannot be wounded with weapons. In the *Sögubrot* Harald's invulnerability is caused by a great working of a type of magic called *seiðr* or "seidh"—and while the *Sögubrot* doesn't mention Odin by name, *Ynglinga saga* reminds us that Odin is a master of seidh, that he can make enemies' weapons fail to bite, and that his chosen warriors could not be wounded by weapons.[56]

Harald is victorious in every battle, and he lives to a great age, but at the end of his life, decrepit and crippled, he decides that he wants to die fighting. He vows all those who are slain on the battlefield—a stupendously large number of heroes and champions—as a great sacrifice to Odin. And although the *Sögubrot* does not state that Odin himself kills Harald, Saxo is clear that Odin claims him after granting him one last great fight, striking him down with a club since blades cannot cut him. Snorri Sturluson wrote a verse that, while actually commenting on the politics of his day, suggests that it was widely understood that Odin instigated the battle of Brávellir:

> The sole shaper of spell-songs°   *sole shaper of spell-songs*: Odin
> summoned Hring and Wartooth
> to the din of plunder°. Gaut° drove them   *din of plunder*: battle; *Gaut*: Odin
> to dispute in battle.[57]

Fighting on the other side is Starkad, whose destiny has been shaped by both Odin and Thor; in some ways he appears as another "Odinnic hero", but as Dumézil points out, he also has Thor-like traits and may originally have been a "Thorian hero".[58] *Gautreks saga*[59] tells of his early life; as a young man, he was fostered by a man named Hrósshárgrani ("Horsehair-Grani") who turned out to be Odin in disguise. At a council of the gods, Thor, who held a grudge against Starkad's family, cursed him, but Odin gave blessings to counter the curses. Thus Thor deemed that Starkad would have no descendants; Odin gave him a lifespan equal to three normal lives; Thor countered that he would commit a vile deed in each lifetime. Odin blessed him with the best of weapons and clothes; Thor cursed him to never be satisfied; Odin blessed him with victory in every battle; Thor countered that he would always be terribly wounded; Odin blessed him with poetic skill; Thor countered that he would never remember his own poems; Odin blessed him with great riches and the esteem of the nobles; Thor cursed him to never own land and to be hated by commoners. Both blessings and curses play out to the fullest in Starkad's life, as he travels the known world, doing deeds of great valor and serving many kings. Like Harald, Starkad gets his last great fight at Bravellir; he survives, but is left crippled and maimed. Soon after, he pays a bystander to kill him.

Saxo calls Starkad's killer Hatherus—a name that quite possibly is a version of Höðr, Balder's slayer, as Dumézil suggests[60]. Höðr is blind in Snorri's telling of the myth of Balder—and Odin himself has names that refer to his weak eyesight, including *Tvíblindi* ("blind in both eyes") and *Bileygr* ("weak eyes"). This has suggested to many scholars that Höðr is a reflection of Odin himself, and that in the oldest version of the myth, Odin caused Balder to be sacrificed.[61] Balder was probably not originally the mild and passive figure that Snorri makes him in his *Edda*; his name means "ruler", and he dies as a *heilagr tafn* or "holy sacrifice" (as the skald Úlfr Uggason called him). In the *Sögubrot*, perhaps, Balder's myth may be reflected in the life and death of Harald Wartooth and Starkad. Odin has made Harald invulnerable, as Balder was made invulnerable, and granted Harald and Starkad victory in every battle—and in the end, he himself must come to claim their lives as sacrifices.

Ragnar

Ragnar Lodbrok—*Ragnarr Loðbrók*, in Old Norse—stands at the farthest edge of history. Although there is no definitive proof that he existed, he is often identified with a Viking leader whose forces sacked Paris in 845, named *Reginheri* in Frankish chronicles (although the sagas of Ragnar Lodbrok do not specifically state that he himself ever raided in the Frankish kingdom). Ragnar may also be the *Raginarius* who was given land and a monastery by the Frankish king Charles the Bald in 840.[62] The chronicles claim that he and most of his men died or were stricken soon after his raid in 845, as divine retribution for plundering Christian holy sites[63], which does not fit the legendary story of Ragnar Lodbrok. That said, the chronicles could be in error, perhaps reporting his death for propagandistic reasons. If that's the case, there may be evidence that Ragnar may have gone on to raid in Ireland, dying there sometime between 852 and 856. His sagas don't mention Ireland, but *Krákumál* depicts him as active there; Saxo Grammaticus claims that he raided in Ireland; and Irish chronicles record a major invasion of Norsemen beginning in 851. These chronicles record a Norse king named *Ragnall*, who could conceivably have been the same person as Reginheri; alternatively, Reginheri and Ragnall could have been separate persons, conflated in the figure of Ragnar Lodbrok. The story of Ragnar's last raids and death, which unlike his sons' invasion cannot be traced in the *Anglo-Saxon Chronicle*, may have been transferred to northern England in the *Saga* and the *Þáttr*.[64]

The sources give different lists of Ragnar's sons. The *Tale of Ragnar's Sons* mentions Eirek and Agnar by his first wife, and Ivar, Bjorn, Hvitserk and Sigurd by his second. *The Saga of Ragnar Lodbrok* adds Rognvald to the list, and Saxo Grammaticus's *History of the Danes* adds several more, including a son named Ubbi, by a concubine. Several people with those names lived at the right time and place, claimed or were reputed to be his sons, and did some of the deeds mentioned in these sources. Adam of Bremen mentions "Ingvar, the son of Lodbrok, who everywhere tortured Christians to death"[65]. Some manuscripts of the *Anglo-Saxon Chronicle* name Ivar and Ubbi as the leaders of the invading Great Heathen Army[66]; Asser's *Life of King Alfred* specifically names "Lodobroch" as the father of Ivar and Ubbi.[67] Bjorn Ironsides appears under the Latinized name *Bier costae ferrae* in the chronicle of William of Jumiéges, who adds that he was the son of "Lodparch"; his forces raided in France in 856-857, and he led a fleet to the Mediterranean, attacking towns in Spain, south France, and north Italy, from 858 to 862.[68] Yet another Frankish chronicle, the *Annales Fuldenses*, mentions the Viking leader Sigifridus, killed at the Dijle River, whom the *Tale of Ragnar's Sons* identifies as Sigurd Snake-in-the-Eye.[69] The *Anglo-Saxon Chronicle*, Frankish chronicles, and possibly some Irish texts mention a presumed brother of Ivar and Sigurd named Halfdan[70]; he is not mentioned in the sagas, but it's conceivable that he could be identified with Hvitserk, whose name ("white shirt") could originally have been a nickname.

This is the shaky historical core that lies at the center of a mass of legends and folktales, which have been shaped to conform to the pattern of a hero's life found widely in folklore. To give a few examples: Ragnar's stratagem of wearing shaggy clothes smeared with tar has parallels from as far away as Russia and Persia; a Russian folktale, for example, has a cobbler protect himself from a great serpent by wrapping himself in flax and smearing it with tar[71]. The *Saga*'s story of Ragnar's challenge to Aslaug/Kraka—come neither naked nor clad, neither sated nor hungry, neither alone nor in company—is a widespread motif, found in tales ranging from Grimm's "The Peasant's Wise Daughter", to some versions of the Irish tale of Diarmuid and Grainné, to "The Chick-Pea Seller's Daughter" in the *Arabian Nights*.[72] Kraka's own history is a version of the "Persecuted Heroine" folktale, like Cinderella or Cap o'Rushes.[73]

The *Saga* mentions how Ivar's body protects Britain from invasion as long as it rests in its mound; this may well have been borrowed from Celtic myth, such as the Welsh legend of Bendigeid Bran's head buried at London. The detail that Ivar's body remained undecayed in its tomb could have been taken from any number of Christian saints' lives, however unsaintly Ivar seems. Finally, some aspects of the Völsung legend have been grafted onto the tale of Ragnar—in fact, the version of the *Saga* that is translated here was written as a continuation of the *Völsunga saga*. In both the *Saga* and the *Tale*, Ragnar's second wife is Aslaug, the daughter of Sigurd the Völsung and Brynhild—which can't be historically accurate, since, to the extent that we can date them at all, Sigurd and Brynhild would have lived about 350 years before Ragnar. Ragnar's death in King Ælla's snakepit was probably borrowed from the story of Gunnar's death in Atli's snakepit.

Several chronicles refer to "sons of Lodbrok", but only the Norse sources identify Loðbrók with Ragnar, and the earliest text to equate Ragnar and Lodbrok dates from 1070. Other sources don't state explicitly that Ragnar and Lodbrok are the same person. Rory McTurk has presented a long argument that Loðbrók was originally a female name[74]; he compares it with *Loðkona*, the name of a presumed goddess known only from a place-name, whose name means something like "woman of growth".[75] In support of this idea, McTurk cites a rune inscription left behind by Norsemen who broke into the chambered tomb at Maes Howe, Orkney, in the mid-12th century: "This mound was built before Loðbrók's. Her sons, they were bold; such were men, as they were of themselves [i.e., they were the sort of people you would really call men]."[76] This inscription is clearly carved, and definitely refers to Lodbrok as female, although it's possible that the rune-carvers made a mistake or were cracking a joke.

Thus the legends of Ragnar and his family are very much a patchwork—a dimly visible historical core, covered by a mass of folktales and legends. Yet the saga-writers didn't perceive his story as "legend" or "myth" in the modern sense; they connected Ragnar's life and deeds to the world they knew. In fact, if later sagas and historical sources are to be believed, some Norsemen found the tale of Ragnar and his kin to be a justification for their territorial expansion. The *Sögubrot* tells of Ragnar's great-grandfather, the legendary king Ívarr *viðfaðmi* (Ivar Wide-Grasp), who ruled an empire that included all Scandinavia and northern England. The *Sögubrot* adds that Ragnar's father, Sigurd Hring, lost England when he became too old to defend his kingdom. Ragnar says explicitly in Chapter II of the *Tale* that "I have now won back under my rule almost all the kingdom that my ancestors had, except for England", before sailing off on his disastrous invasion. Several other legendary sagas perpetrate this myth of the "Viking Empire"—an ancient kingdom reaching from England to Russia.[77]

Even if Ragnar and his ancestors are partly—or wholly—fictional, the myth of the "Viking Empire" provided inspiration and justification for Norsemen who had designs on the north of England. In *Jómsvíkinga saga*, Ragnar's descendants Knut and Harald invade northern England around the year 940 because "they claimed it as their inheritance, because the sons of Lodbrók and other forebears of theirs had possessed it."[78] And the myth lasted a long time; Norse rule over parts of northern England lasted from the coming of the "sons of Lodbrok" and their Great Heathen Army in 865, to 954, when Eirik Bloodaxe was driven out. It resumed in 1013, when Svein Forkbeard drove out Æthelred the Unready; Harald Hardrada tried to press his own claim in 1066, and the Danes invaded England and captured York again in 1069. Norse claims to more northerly parts of Britain lasted even longer: the Norwegian kingdom didn't formally relinquish its claims in northern Scotland and the Hebrides until 1266. There were plenty of reasons why the Norse kept invading Britain, but it's not a stretch at all to suggest that, as the descendants of these heroes of old, they must have felt that their cause was just.

Notes on the Texts and Translations

My translations from Norse were originally made from the texts printed in the three-volume set *Fornaldarsögur Norðurlanda*, edited by Guðni Jónsson and Bjarni Vilhjálmsson. I have checked my translations against the critical editions of the *Sögubrot* and parts of the *Þáttr af Ragnars sonum* published in *Danakonunga sögur*, edited by Bjarni Guðnason, in the *Íslenzk fornrit* series. This volume also includes the Latin text of the extract from the *List of Swedish Kings*.

There are two surviving manuscripts of the *Saga of Ragnar Lodbrok* (*Ragnars saga loðbrókar*). This translation follows the most complete manuscript (NkS 1824b 4to), written around 1400 and preserved in the Royal Danish Library. This manuscript also includes *Völsunga saga*, and presents *Ragnars saga* as a direct continuation of *Völsunga saga*, which explains its rather abrupt beginning. The other manuscript (AM 147 4to) presents a slightly different version of events; unfortunately, it is incomplete. Both versions are thought to descend from a lost text known as the **Original Saga of Ragnar Lodbrok*, which would have been composed around 1230.[79] The last published English translation of this saga was made by Margaret Schlauch and printed in 1930.[80]

The next three texts are connected, not simply by subject matter, but because they all draw on the *Skjöldunga saga*, whose complete Norse text is lost. The *Sögubrot* ("Saga Fragment") is thought to be a fragment of a late version of the *Skjöldunga saga*, to which material had been added that was not present in earlier recensions. The manuscript is catalogued as AM 1 e β I fol. in the Arnamagnæan Institute, at the University of Copenhagen. The beginning and end of the manuscript are illegible, and the middle two pages are also missing.

In 1596, the Icelandic historian Arngrímr Jónsson wrote a Latin version of the still-extant *Skjöldunga saga*, filling in gaps in his copy of the saga with other materials and adding his own commentary. The largest portion is now known as *Rerum Danicarum fragmenta* (*Fragments of the Deeds of the Danes*); it begins with the god Odin and breaks off generations before Ragnar.[81] *Ad catalogum regum Sveciæ annotanda* (*List of Swedish Kings*) is another section of Arngrímr's manuscript, which preserves a portion of the *Skjöldunga saga* that does include Ragnar and his close kin. There has been some debate as to just how faithful Arngrímr's version is to the original Norse; he may have abridged it considerably, or else he may have made a fairly accurate translation of a shorter recension of the original saga.[82] Arngrímr's original manuscript was lost in a fire, but a copy was made, and this is bound with other works by Arngrímr in Volume XXV of the Thomas Bartholin collection of manuscripts, now in the Royal Danish Library (shelfmark Don. var. 1 fol. Barth. XXV). It should be obvious from the texts in this volume that the *List of Swedish Kings* overlaps with the end of *Sögubrot* and the beginning of the *Tale of Ragnar's Sons*.

The *Tale of Ragnar's Sons* (*Þáttr af Ragnars sonum*) is found only in *Hauksbók*, written in the early 1300s by the Icelander Haukr Erlendsson, also known as Haukr *lögrmaðr* (Hauk the Lawman). *Hauksbók* is an eclectic compilation of texts that Haukr copied himself or had copied for him. In addition to Christian writings, historical works, and mathematical texts, *Hauksbók* contains several sagas, tales, and historical works. The author of the tale in the form we have it, who may or may not have been Haukr himself, seems to have combined material from the **Original Saga of Ragnar Lodbrok* with material from the *Skjöldunga saga*, abridging both sources somewhat.[83] In the 1600s, *Hauksbók* was disbound and split up; the section containing *Þáttr af Ragnars sonum* is now catalogued as AM 544 4to in the Arnamagnæan Institute.[84]

Krákumál appears in several manuscripts; the most complete version is in the same manuscript that contains the complete version of the *Saga of Ragnar Lodbrok*, NkS 1824b 4to. It is an example of a "life-poem" (*ævikviða*), in which the speaker reviews the deeds of his life, often as he is dying. Several such poems are found in *fornaldarsögur*, notably *Örvar-Odds saga* and *Hervarar saga*, and similar poems exist in other early Germanic languages, such as Beowulf's death-speech in *Beowulf*.[85]

Krákumál may have been composed in Orkney or Scotland; not only is the style similar to that of known skalds in Orkney such as Jarl Rögnvaldr Kali, but many of the place-names, not known from the prose sagas, suggest that Ragnar's career of raiding began in Scandinavia but moved on to Scotland, then to Ireland and Wales.[86] The prose sagas don't mention Ragnar raiding in this region, but Saxo's *History of the Danes* mentions several episodes of raiding here; both *Krákumál* and Saxo may have drawn on traditions that the saga compilers were not aware of.

There has been a long and involved debate as to whether the sagas were primarily derived from oral tradition ("free-prose") or from written literary tradition ("book-prose"); the best answer seems to be that many sagas are a complex mixture of both. But sagas were often read aloud as entertainment in Iceland, not just in medieval times but as late as the early 20th century. Furthermore, many features of Old Norse saga style do not make for easily readable English if translated literally. Verb tenses flip back and forth from present tense to past; passive constructions abound, such as "and so it was done, that" and "it seemed to him that he knew that"; and repeated independent clauses beginning with conjunctions are typical: "And.... And then... But then... And so..." Any translator must make a judgment call on how much to "smooth out" the prose; while there has been a long trend away from the archaisms and calques of Victorian translators towards more plain and colloquial language, the pendulum may be beginning to swing the other way.[87] Instead of trying to catch every last twist of the Norse, I've tried to stay true to the original meaning while also creating something that will work well as spoken prose—to capture something of the flavor of a tale that might have told around a fire in the depths of winter (with periodic questions, comments, and even heckling from the audience—which the reader may freely supply).

The poetic stanzas are especially difficult to translate. Most of them are written in variants of skaldic forms (although not the most elaborate forms possible), in which there is a strict syllable count and rhyme scheme, in addition to the alliteration that is basic to old Germanic poetry. *Heiti* (poetic synonyms) and *kenningar* (metaphorical figures of speech) abound in skaldic poetry, and word order is extremely flexible. Some stanzas could be—and have been!—translated in more than one way, and in fact may have been meant to have multiple meanings. I haven't even tried to duplicate this formal complexity. I've maintained as much alliteration as I thought possible, and tried to stay close to the six-syllable, three-stress half-lines of skaldic poetry, but I haven't hesitated to break these rules when any alternative seemed excessively stilted.

Introduction

I thank Steven Abell, Dan Campbell, Julie Coleman, Diana Paxson, Amanda Waggoner, and Lorrie Wood for their encouragement and for commenting on these translations in various drafts. I also thank Zoe Borovsky, Sean Crist, P. S. Langeslag, Stefan Langeslag, Andy Lemons, Carsten Lyngdrup Madsen, and Jon Julius Sandal, who have created freely available electronic resources that were absolutely crucial for my work; and Chris Van Dyke[88] and Peter Tunstall[89], whose online translations were useful in clarifying textual points and correcting some of my worst errors. Any remaining mistakes are entirely my own fault.

Hvárt sem satt er eða eigi,
þá hafi sa gaman af, er þat má at verða,
en hinir leiti annars þess gamans, er þeim þykkir betra.

SAGA OF RAGNAR LODBROK AND HIS SONS

CHAPTER I

In Hlymdal, Heimir heard the news that Sigurd and Brynhild were dead.[1] Aslaug, their daughter and Heimir's foster-daughter, was three years old then. He now knew that enemies would seek to destroy the girl and all her family. But he grieved so much over the death of Brynhild, his foster-daughter, that he cared neither for his own kingdom nor his wealth. He realized that he could not keep the girl there in secret. He had a harp made that was so large that he put the girl Aslaug inside it, along with many precious objects of gold and silver.[2] Then he went away and traveled widely throughout the land, and at last came to the Northlands. His harp was so skillfully made that he could take it apart and put it together at the joints, and on days when he came to waterfalls with no houses nearby, it was his custom to take the harp apart and bathe the girl. He had a wine-leek[3] which he gave her to eat—the nature of this leek is such that a person may survive for a long time, even if he has no other food. And when the girl cried, he would strike up his harp and she would quiet down, for Heimir was accomplished at those skills which were practiced at the time. He also had many costly clothes in the harp with her, and much gold.

Now he traveled until he reached Norway, and he came to a little farm that was called Spangareid[4]. An old man named Aki lived there. He had a wife, and she was called Grima. There were no more people than themselves. That day, the old man had gone to the forest, but the old woman was home. She greeted Heimir and asked who he was. He said that he was a beggar, and asked the old woman for shelter. She said that no one else came there, so she could welcome him, if he thought he needed to stay.

In the end, he said that he would be most comfortable if he could sit before a fire, and then be shown to quarters where he might sleep. When the old woman had kindled the fire, he set the harp up and set it next to himself. The old woman was speaking excitedly; her gaze often lit on the harp, because the fringe on a luxurious piece of clothing was hanging out of the harp. And as he warmed himself by the fire, she saw a costly gold ring sticking out from under his rags, because he was poorly dressed.

When he had warmed himself as much as he felt that he needed, then he had supper. After that, he asked the old woman to show him to the place where he should sleep that night. The old woman said that he would be better off outside the house than in, "because my husband and I often talk a lot when he comes home." He asked her to decide.

Then he went outside and so did she. He took the harp and kept it with him. The old woman went out to where there was a barley barn. She guided him there and said that he should settle down there, and said that she hoped that he would enjoy his sleep. And now the old woman went away and busied herself with the work she had to do, and he got ready for sleep.

The old man came home as evening was coming on. The old woman had worked very little at what she needed to do. He was tired and grouchy when he came home, when everything that she should have worked at was undone. The old man said that there must be a great difference in their happiness, since he worked every day, more than he was able, but she didn't feel like doing anything useful.

"Don't be angry, my husband", she said, "because you may be able to work for just a little while to make the two of us happy all our lives."

"What is it?" said the old man.

The old woman answered, "A man has come to our lodgings, and I think he has plenty of money with him for traveling. He is bent by old age, but he must have been the greatest of champions once, yet now he's very weary. I don't think that I've ever seen anyone like him, but I think that he's exhausted and asleep."

Then the old man said, "I don't think it's right to betray the few people who come here."

She answered, "That's why you'll always be a weakling: everything looks too big to you. Now do one of two things: you kill him, or I'll take him for my own husband and we'll drive you away. I can tell you the words that he said to me this evening, though they'll seem unworthy to you. He spoke seductively to me. That will be my plan: to take him as my own man, and drive you away or kill you, if you won't do what I want."

It's said that the old man was ruled by his wife, and she talked until he gave in to her egging him on. He took his axe and sharpened it a great deal. When he was ready, the old woman led him to where Heimir was sleeping. He was snoring loudly. Then the old woman said to the old man that he should make his attack as best he could—"and get away quickly, because you won't be able to withstand his bellowing and shouting, once he gets his hands on you." She took the harp and ran off with it.

Now the old man came up to where Heimir was sleeping. He struck at him and gave him a great wound, and the axe got loose from him. He ran away from there as fast as he could. Heimir awoke at the blow, and that was quite enough for him. It is said that his death-throes made such a great din that the pillars of the house fell down and the entire house collapsed and there was a great earthquake, and there he lost his life.

Now the old man came to the old woman and said that he had killed him—"though for a moment I didn't know how it would go. This man was incredibly mighty, but I suppose that he is now in Hel."

The old woman said that he would have her thanks for the deed—"and I expect that now we two will have enough money. We'll find out whether I have spoken the truth."

Now they kindled a fire, and the old woman took the harp and tried to open it. She couldn't get it open in any other way than breaking it, because she didn't have the skill. But once she got the harp opened up, there she saw a girl-child, and she thought that she had never seen anyone like her. There was also much money in the harp.

Now the old man said, "This will now turn out as it often does. When someone betrays the one who trusted him, it ends badly. It seems that we have a dependent on our hands."

The old woman answered, "This is not going as I had planned, but no harm will come of it." And now she asked the girl what family she came from. But to this the young girl gave no answer, as if she had not learned speech.

"Now our plan will turn out badly, just as I expected", said the old man. "We two have committed a great crime. How can we provide for this child?"

"That's obvious," said Grima. "She shall be named Kraka[5], after my mother."

Now the old man said, "How will we provide for this child?"

The old woman replied, "I see a good plan. We will say that she is our daughter and raise her."

"No one will believe that," said the old man. "This child is much more attractive than we are. We're both completely ugly, and it won't seem likely that the two of us would have such a child, as horrid as we both are."

The old woman said, "You don't know this, but I have a certain trick to make her seem ugly. I will shave her head, and smear it with tar and other things when her hair is likely to grow back. She shall wear a hood after that. She will also not be well dressed. Then she will take on our appearance. Maybe people will believe that I was very beautiful when I was young. And she shall do the worst chores."

The old man and woman thought that she could not speak, for she never answered them. Now everything was done as the old woman had planned, and she grew up there in great poverty.

CHAPTER II

Herrud was the name of a powerful and famous jarl in Gautland. He was married. His daughter was named Thora. She was the loveliest of all women in appearance, and the most well-mannered, in every possible respect that is better to have than to be without. She was called Fortress-Hart as a nickname, because she excelled all women in beauty, as much as the hart excels over other animals. The jarl greatly loved his daughter. He had a bower made for her, separate from the king's hall, and around that bower was a plank fence.

The jarl made it his habit to send his daughter something for her amusement every day, and he said that he would continue to do so. Concerning that, it's said that he had a little heather-snake brought to her one day, impressively beautiful.[6] This snake pleased her, and she kept it in her little box and placed a piece of gold under it. It had only been there a short while before it had grown greatly, and so had the gold underneath it. Then the day came when it had no room inside the box, and it lay in a ring around the box. And it happened later that it had no room in the bower—and the gold grew underneath it, just as much as the serpent itself. Now it lay outside, around the bower, so that it put its head and tail together, and it became hard to deal with. No one dared to come to the bower because of this serpent, except for the person who brought its food—and it required an ox for every meal.[7] This seemed to the jarl to be a great harm, and he swore this oath that he would give his daughter to that man, whomever he might be, who could kill the serpent, and the gold that was under it should be her dowry. This news spread far and wide throughout the land, but no one trusted himself to prevail over this great serpent.

CHAPTER III

At that time, Sigurd Hring ruled over Denmark. He was a mighty king and had become famous from the battle that he had fought against Harald Wartooth at Bravellir. Harald fell before him, as has become known in all the northern lands of the world.[8]

Sigurd had one son, who was called Ragnar. He was grown to great size, handsome in appearance and keen in understanding, generous to his men and fierce to his enemies. As soon as he was old enough, he got himself some men and a warship, and became the greatest warrior, so that hardly anybody was a match for him. He heard what Jarl Herrud had spoken about; he paid no attention and acted as if he didn't know. He had some clothes made for himself, with a strange appearance; they were shaggy breeches and a shaggy cape, and once they were made, he had them boiled in tar.[9] Then he hid them.

5

One summer, he led his forces to Gautland, and laid up one of his ships in a hidden inlet. It was a short way from there to where the jarl ruled. When Ragnar had been there one night, he awoke early in the morning, got up and put on the same protective clothes that were mentioned before, and he took a large spear in his hand. He went alone from the ships to where there was sand, and he rolled in the sand. Before he went away, he took the rivet out of his spear.

Now he went alone from the ships to the gate of the jarl's fortress, and arrived there so early in the day that all the men were asleep. He headed for the bower. And when he came to the enclosure where the serpent was, he stabbed at it with his spear, and then he quickly pulled the spear back. He stabbed again. That thrust went into the serpent's spine. Then he twisted the spear quickly, so that the spearpoint came off the shaft. The serpent's death struggles made such a great din that all the bower shook.

Now Ragnar turned away. Then a gush of blood struck him between his shoulders, but that didn't hurt him—the clothes that he had made had protected him that well. Those who were in the bower awoke from the noise and came out of the bower. Thora saw a large man walking away from the bower, and asked him what his name was and what he had come for. He stopped and spoke this verse:

> I've gambled my glorious life,
> girl of fair complexion,
> fought the fish of the land°,
> though fifteen winters old.
> I have conquered, cleaving
> the coiled heath-salmon° to the heart—
> unless its bale should bite,
> bringing me sudden death.

fish of the land: serpent

heath-salmon: serpent

Then he went away and said nothing more to her. The spearpoint stayed behind in the wound, but he kept the shaft with him. Now that she had heard this verse, she understood what he said about his mission, and how old he was. She wondered to herself who he might be, and she wasn't sure whether he was human or not, because his size, for his age, seemed to her to be as large as was said about monsters. She turned back into the bower and went to sleep.

When the people came out in the morning, they realized that the serpent was lying there dead, with a great spearpoint sticking fast in the wound. The jarl had the spearpoint taken out, and it was so large that few could wield it. Now the jarl mused on what he had said concerning the man who would slay the serpent. He wasn't sure whether a human being had wielded that spear or not.

6

Now he discussed, with his friends and daughter, how he should look for the man. They though it likely that that man would seek the reward which he had won. She advised him to have all the people summoned to an assembly—"and command that all men should come there who don't want to provoke the jarl's anger, and who in any way are able to answer the summons. If there is anyone who will avow the serpent's death-wound, he will have that spearshaft which fits the point." This seemed like a good idea to the jarl, and he had the assembly proclaimed. And when the day arrived, the jarl came, and many other chieftains. A great many people were there.

CHAPTER IV

The news was heard on Ragnar's ship, not far from where the assembly had been summoned. Now Ragnar went with all his men from his ship to the assembly. When they came there, they took places somewhat apart from the other men, because Ragnar now saw that a huge crowd had come, larger than usual.

Then the jarl stood up and called for a hearing. He spoke to thank the people for having responded so well to his message, and then he told of the events that had happened. First he spoke about his promise concerning that man who should slay the serpent. Then he said, "The serpent is now dead, and the man who has accomplished this glorious deed has left the spearhead behind, sticking in the wound. If anyone has come here to the assembly who has the shaft that fits this spearhead, let him bring it forward and let him prove his report in this way. Then I shall fulfill all that I have promised, whether the man be of higher or lower degree." And he concluded his speech by having the spearhead borne before each man who was at the assembly, and he ordered that whosoever should avow the deed, and had that shaft which fit, should speak up. And so it was done. Not a one was found who had the shaft.

Then the spearhead was brought to where Ragnar was, and shown to him. He avowed that it was his, and the shaft and the spearhead fit each other.[10] The men realized that he must have been the serpent's killer, and from this deed he became by far the most famous man in all the Northlands. He asked for Thora the jarl's daughter, and he welcomed her. She was given in marriage to him, and he was given a great feast with the best provisions in the kingdom. At that feast, Ragnar married her. And when the feast was over, Ragnar went to his own kingdom and ruled it, and he loved Thora greatly. They had two sons: the elder was named Eirek, and Agnar was the younger. They were tall in stature and handsome in appearance. They were much stronger than most other men who were around at that time. They learned all kinds of sports and skills.

But one day, Thora felt sick, and she expired from her illness. This was such a great blow to Ragnar that he would not rule the kingdom and appointed other men to rule the kingdom with his sons. He now took up the same occupation that he had had before, and began raiding. Wherever he went, he won victory.

CHAPTER V

One summer, he set his ship's course for Norway, because he had many kinsmen and friends there and wanted to meet them. He came in his ship at evening to a little harbor. There was a farm, which was called Spangareid, a short way from there.

Ragnar's men laid up there in the anchorage that night, and when morning came, the cooks had to go on land to bake bread. They saw that the farm was a short way ahead of them, and it seemed to them that it was more suitable to go to the house and work there. When they came to this little farm, they met a person having a meal, and it was an old woman. They asked whether she was the lady of the house, and what her name was. She said that she was the lady of the house—"and my name's not lacking, I'm called Grima, but who are you?"

They said that they were the servants of Ragnar Lodbrok, and they wanted to be about their business—"and we want you to work with us." The old woman answered that her hands were very stiff. "But formerly I could do my work well enough, and I have myself a daughter who will work with you. She'll come home soon. Her name is Kraka. Things have gotten to the point now that I can hardly manage to control her."

Now Kraka had gone with the livestock in the morning, and she saw that many large ships had come to the land. She began to wash herself—though the old woman had forbidden her to do that, because she didn't want for men to see her beauty, for she was the loveliest of all women. Her hair was so long that it touched the ground behind her, and as fair as the finest silk.[11]

Then Kraka came home. The cooks had made a fire, and Kraka saw that men had come whom she had not seen before. She looked at them, and they looked at her. And then they asked Grima, "Is that beautiful girl your daughter?"

"It's no lie," said Grima, "she is my daughter."

"You two must be incredibly unlike", they said, "as hideous as you are. We have never seen a maiden so beautiful, and we don't think that she looks anything like you, because you are the greatest monstrosity."

Grima answered, "You can't see the resemblance in me now. My looks aren't what they used to be."

Now they decided that Kraka should work with them. She asked, "What shall I do?" They said that they wanted her to knead the bread, and they then would bake it. She took up her task, and did it well. But they kept turning to stare at her, so that they paid no attention to their job and burned the bread.

When they had finished their work, they returned to the ship. And when they had to serve the ship's mess, everyone said that they had never done such a poor job, and deserved punishment. Ragnar asked why they had prepared the food that way. They said that they had seen a woman so lovely that they paid no attention to their work, and they supposed that there could be no one more beautiful in the world. When they had finished saying so much about her beauty, Ragnar said that he knew that she could not be as beautiful as Thora had been. They said that she was no less beautiful.

Then Ragnar said, "Now I will send men who know how to see clearly. If it is as you say, then your carelessness is forgiven, but if the woman is in any way less beautiful than you have said, you will bring down great punishment on yourselves." And he sent his men to meet this fair maiden, but the headwind was so great that they could not go that day.

Ragnar said to his messengers, "If this young maiden seems as lovely to you as has been reported, ask her to come to meet me, and I will meet with her; I want her to be mine. But I want for her to be neither clad nor unclad, neither sated nor hungry, and for her not to come alone, yet no one may come with her."[12]

Now they traveled until they came to the house, and they observed Kraka carefully, and the woman seemed so lovely to them that they thought that no other was as beautiful. Then they told her the message from their lord Ragnar, about how she should be prepared. Kraka thought about what the king had said, and how she should prepare herself, but Grima thought there was no way that this could be done, and she said that she knew that this king could not be wise. Kraka said, "He must have said this because it can be done, if we can figure out what he meant. But I certainly cannot travel with you today. I will come to your ship early in the morning." Then they went away and told Ragnar how it was arranged that she would come to meet them.

Kraka stayed at home that night. But early in the morning, she said to the old man that she had go to meet Ragnar. "But I must alter my costume somewhat. You have a fishing net for trout, and I will wrap that around myself, and let my hair fall down over it, and then I will be bare nowhere.[13] I will taste a leek, and that is little food, but yet he will recognize that I have eaten. And I must have your dog follow me, and then I won't go alone, yet no person will come with me."

When the old woman heard her plans, she realized that she was very intelligent. And when Kraka was ready, she went on her way until she came to the ship. Her appearance was lovely, and her hair was as bright as gold.

Ragnar called to her and asked who she might be and whom she wanted to meet. She replied with a verse:

> I don't dare to refuse
> the decree that I must come,
> nor break with your bidding
> to be here, lord Ragnar.
> No man stands beside me,
> and my skin is not bare;
> I have my fine following,
> though I fared here alone.

Now he sent men to meet her and had them lead her onto his ship. But she said that she didn't want to go unless she and her fellow traveler were granted safe conduct. Then she was led onto the king's ship, and when she came onto the deck, Ragnar reached out his hands to her, but the dog bit his hand. His men rushed at the dog and beat it and throttled it with a bowstring, and that killed it—she got no better safe conduct than that!

Ragnar seated her on the afterdeck next to himself and talked with her. She suited his mind well, and he was happy with her. He spoke a verse:

> If the fatherland's defender°   *fatherland's defender*: king (i.e. Ragnar)
> to the fine lady were kind,
> truly she would take me
> tenderly in her arms.

She said:

> If you respect safe conduct,
> surely you will let me go
> home from here, unblemished—
> though a helmsman° I have sought.   *helmsman*: king

CHAPTER VI

He now said that he was pleased with her, and he truly wanted her to come with him. She said that that could not be. Then he said that he wanted her to be there on his ship that night. She said that that could not happen before he returned from the journey that he had intended—"and it may be that by then, something else will seem better to you."

10

Then Ragnar called his treasurer and asked him to take a shirt that Thora had owned, all embroidered with gold, and present it to her.[14] Ragnar offered it to Kraka in this way:

Will you take this shirt,
which Thora Hart once had?
Sewn about with silver,
it suits you very well.
Her pale hands once passed
over this precious garment;
she was kind until death
to this king of blithe heroes.

Kraka replied:

I don't dare take the shirt
which Thora Hart once had,
sewn about with silver—
what suits me is shabby clothing,
for I am called Kraka,
in coal-black clothes,
who goes over the gravel,
driving goats with me.

"And I certainly don't want to accept the shirt," she sad. "I won't dress myself in finery while I live with the old man. It may be that you would like me better if I dressed myself better. I want to go home now. But you may send men after me, if you still have the same thing in mind and you want me to go with you."

Ragnar said that he would not change his mind, and she went home. Ragnar and his men left as they had planned, as soon as they had a favorable wind, and he discharged his errands as he had intended. When he returned, he came to the same harbor where he had been before, when Kraka came to him. That same evening he sent men to find her and give her Ragnar's message that she should leave now for good. But she said that she could not leave before morning.

Kraka got up early and went to the old couple's bed and asked whether they were awake. They said that they were awake and asked what she wanted. She said that she intended to go away and stay there no longer. "I know that you killed Heimir, my foster-father, and I want to pay back no one but you. For the sake of the long time that I have lived with you two, I will not do you any harm—but I now pronounce that each day will be worse for you than those that have passed, and your last day will be the worst. Now we are parted."

11

Then she went on her way to the ships and was welcomed warmly. They had good weather. That same evening, when the men had to make up their beds, Ragnar said that he wanted them to sleep together. She said that that could not be—"and I want you to hold a wedding-feast for me[15] when you come to your kingdom. That seems to me to be honorable, for me as well as for you, and for our heirs, if we should have any." He granted her this favor, and they traveled well.

Ragnar now came home to his own land, and a lavish feast was spread for him, and both the welcoming-ale in his honor and his wedding-ale were drunk. And the first evening that they shared a bed, Ragnar wanted to couple with his wife, but she excused herself, because she said that she would suffer consequences if she didn't get her way. Ragnar said that he could not believe that, and he said that the old man and woman couldn't see the future. He asked how long they should wait. She said:

> For three nights, we two—
> though together in the hall—
> shall sleep separately, ere
> we sacrifice to holy gods.
> This delay will do no
> damage to my child;
> you're brash to beget one
> whose bones will be lacking.

Although she said that, Ragnar gave it no heed and disregarded her advice.[16]

CHAPTER VII

Now time went by, and their marriage was good and very loving. Kraka found that she was pregnant, and gave birth to a boy-child. The boy was sprinkled with water and given the name Ivar.[17] But the boy was boneless, as if there were gristle where his bones should be.[18] When he was young, he was grown so large that no one was his equal. He was the handsomest of all men, and so wise that it wasn't certain whether there had ever been a wiser man than him.

They were destined to have more children. Their second son was named Bjorn, the third was Hvitserk, and the fourth was Rognvald. They were all great men and the most valiant. As soon as they could do anything, they took up all sorts of sports. And wherever they went, Ivar had them carry him on poles, because he couldn't walk. He would make plans for what they should do.

Now Eirek and Agnar, Ragnar's sons, were such great and mighty men that their equals could hardly be found. They readied their warships every summer and were renowned for their raiding. And one day, Ivar was discussing with his brothers, Hvitserk and Bjorn, how much longer they would sit at home and not seek any fame for themselves. They said that they would act on his advice, in that as in other things. Ivar said, "Now I want us to ask for ships, and men so that they may be well crewed. Then I want us to gain wealth and fame for ourselves, if it may happen that way."

When they had discussed this plan among themselves, they said to Ragnar that they wanted him to get them ships, and crews that were experienced at raiding and well prepared for anything. He did what they asked. Once their men were ready, they sailed away from their land. Wherever they battled with men, they got more loot, and they won for themselves both a large host of men and great riches.

Then Ivar said that he wanted them to head for where a more powerful force would challenge them, so they could test their own prowess. They asked where he knew of this possibility, and he named a place called Hvitabaer[19], where sacrifices were made—"many have attempted to conquer it, and none have gained victory". Ragnar had gone there, but had been turned back and accomplished nothing.

"Are the forces there so large and so strong," they said, "or are there other obstacles?"

Ivar said that both very large forces and a great place for sacrifices were there. Of all those who had attacked it, not one had withstood that. They said that he should decide whether they should head for that place or not. But he said that he really wanted to test which might be greater: their own hardiness, or the sorcery[20] of the inhabitants.

CHAPTER VIII

Now they set their course for that place, and when they came to land, they made ready to go ashore. It occurred to them that they needed some men to guard the ships. Rognvald, their brother, was young then, and they didn't think he was ready to run such a great risk as they thought was likely. They left him to watch over the ships, with some men.

Before they left their ships, Ivar said that the townspeople had two cows, and they were young bulls. Men turned and fled from them when they could not withstand their bellowing and their dreadful magic power.[21] Ivar said, "Brace yourselves as best you can, although you feel some unease, because nothing will hurt you." Then they deployed their forces.

As they approached the town, they realized that the people who lived there were about to release the cattle that they worshipped.[22] And when the bulls were let loose, they rushed forward ferociously and bellowed wickedly. Ivar saw that from the shield where he was being carried. He asked his men to fetch him his bow, and they did. Then he shot the evil bulls and killed them both. The enemy which seemed most terrifying was dispelled by his hand.

Now Rognvald began to speak, back at the ships, and he said to his men that they would be lucky to have such entertainment as his brothers were having. "There's no reason why I should stay behind, except that they alone wanted to have the glory. Now we shall all go up." And they did so. When they came upon the armies, Rognvald charged fiercely into the battle, and in the end he was killed. But the brothers broke through into the town, and the battle began again. In the end, the townsmen turned and fled, and they pursued the fleeing men. When they turned back to the town, Bjorn spoke a verse:

> Our blades bit more than theirs,
> our battle-cry was raised—
> I must tell this truly—
> there on the Gnipafjord.
> Let every man who'd like to—
> lads, don't spare your swords now—
> become, before Hvitabaer,
> the bane of a foeman.

And when they came back to the town, they took all the treasure, burned every house in town, and tore down all the walls. Then they sailed their ships away.

CHAPTER IX

The king who ruled Sweden was named Eystein.[23] He was married and had one daughter. Her name was Ingibjorg. She was the fairest and finest of all women. King Eystein was powerful and had many retainers; he was ill-tempered, and yet wise. He had his royal residence at Uppsala. He was a great sacrificer, and at Uppsala at that time, there were so many sacrifices that there have never been more in the Northlands. They had great faith in a certain cow, and they called her Sibilja.[24] She received so many sacrifices that men could not withstand her bellowing. It was the king's custom, when an invasion was expected, that this very same cow went in front of the ranks. So much devilry followed her, that her enemies lost their senses as soon as they heard her: they fought each other and took no heed for themselves. For that reason, Sweden was never subject to invasion, for men didn't dare to test themselves against such overwhelming odds.

King Eystein was good friends with many men and chieftains, and it is said that at that time there was great friendship between Ragnar and King Eystein. It was their custom that, each summer, one of them should go and feast with the other. Now it so happened that Ragnar had to go and feast with King Eystein. When he came to Uppsala, he and his men were well received. And when they began drinking at the start of the evening, the king had his daughter serve drink to himself and to Ragnar. Ragnar's men said among themselves that there was nothing else he should do but ask for King Eystein's daughter, and he should not be married any longer to a peasant's daughter.[25] It happened that one of his men brought this up with him, and in the end, the woman was promised to him, although she would stay betrothed to him for a very long time.

When their feast was ended, Ragnar prepared to go home, and he traveled well. There is nothing to say about his journey until he was only a short distance from his royal seat, when he led his forces into a forest. They came upon a clearing in the forest. Then Ragnar ordered his men to halt and called for a hearing for himself, and then commanded all the men who had been on his voyage to Sweden not to speak about his future plans for marriage with King Eystein's daughter. He gave a strict order about this: if anyone spoke of this matter, he would lose nothing less than his life.

Now that he had said what he wanted to, he went home to his estate. Men rejoiced that he had come back and drank the welcome-ale in his honor. He came to his high-seat, and he had not sat there long before Kraka came into the hall. She came before Ragnar and sat on his knee and laid her arms around his neck and asked, "What is the news?" But he said that he knew of nothing to tell.

When the evening came, the men began drinking, and later they went to sleep. And when Ragnar and Kraka got into bed together, she asked him again for the news, but he said that he knew nothing. Now she wanted to chat more, but he said that he was very sleepy and weary from traveling.

"Now I will tell you the news", she said, "if you don't want to tell me anything."

He asked what it was. "I call it news", she said, "if a woman is promised to a king, but yet some men are saying that he already has another woman."

"Who told you that?" said Ragnar.

"Your men shall keep their lives and limbs, because no man told me this", she said. "You must have seen that three birds were sitting in a tree next to you. They told me this news.[26] I beg you not to try this plan that you have devised. Now I must tell you that I am a king's daughter and not a peasant's, and my father was such a renowned man that his equal has never been attained, and my mother was the loveliest and wisest of all women, and her name will be remembered while the world lasts."

He asked who her father was, if she wasn't the daughter of the poor old man who lived at Spangarheid. She said that she was the daughter of Sigurd Fafnir's-Bane and Brynhild Budli's-Daughter.

Ragnar said, "It seems to me highly unlikely that their daughter would be named Kraka, or that their child would grow up in such poverty as there was at Spangarheid."

Then she answered, "Here is the story," and began to tell the tale of how Sigurd and Brynhild met on the mountain, and how she was begotten. "And when Brynhild gave birth, a name was given to me, and I was called Aslaug." And she told everything that had happened to her since they met the old man.

Ragnar answered, "I am amazed at these wild tales you tell about Aslaug."

She replied, "You know that I am pregnant, and it must be a boy-child that I am carrying. On that child there will be a mark, which will look like a serpent lying in the child's eyes.[27] If this happens as I have said, I ask you not to go to Sweden at the time when you are to marry the daughter of King Eystein. If it fails, then go wherever you will. But I want this child to be named after my father if that mark of glory is in his eyes, as I believe it will be."

The time came when she went into labor and gave birth to a boy-child. Her serving-women took the child and showed him to her. She said that they should bear him to Ragnar and let him see him, and it was done: the young child was brought into the hall and laid on Ragnar's lap. When he saw the boy, he was asked how he would name him.[28] He spoke a verse:

> The child shall be called Sigurd,
> he'll hold court in battles;
> much like his own mother's
> mighty father shall he be.
> Of all Odin's kindred
> he'll be accounted best.
> Showing a snake in his eye,
> he'll be the slayer of many.

Now he took a gold ring off his own hand and gave it to the boy as a name-gift.[29] When he held out his hand with the gold, he touched the boy's back, and Ragnar took that to mean that the boy would hate gold.[30] And now he spoke this verse:

> The dear son of Brynhild's
> daughter, pleasing to heroes,
> has flashing face-stones°   *face-stones:* eyes
> and a most faithful heart;

16

the bringer of bane-fire°   *bane-fire:* sword; its *bringer:* warrior
wins battles by his strength,
Budli's dauntless descendant
disdains the red-gold rings.

And he said further:

I see in no young swain,
except Sigurd alone,
bridles° laid in the bright stones   *bridles:* snakes
of the brow's borderland°;   *stones of brow's borderland:* eyes
the daring beasts' day-diminisher°   *beasts' day-diminisher:* hunter
is discerned by this mark:
the dark forests' ring° flashes   *forests' ring:* serpent
from the fences of his eyelids.°   *fences of eyelids:* eyes

Now he said that they should take the child out to the bower. Then his plan to go to Sweden was broken off. And the lineage of Aslaug was revealed, so that every man knew that she was the daughter of Sigurd Fafnir's-Bane and Brynhild Budli's-Daughter.

CHAPTER X

Now that time had passed when Ragnar had to come to the feast at Uppsala as agreed—but he didn't come. That seemed to King Eystein to be an insult to himself and his daughter, and the kings' friendship was broken off. When Eirek and Agnar, Ragnar's sons, heard that, they made plans together to get a great host for themselves, as large as they could, and raid in Sweden. They got together a large force of men and made their ship ready. They believed that their success would strongly depend on everything going well when the ship set out.

As it happened, when Agnar's ship was launched from the rollers, there was a man in front of it, and he was killed. They called that the "roller-red". Now it seemed to them that things had not gone well at the start, but they didn't want to let that stand in the way of their journey. And when their forces were ready, they went with their men to Sweden, and they bore the war-shields[31] where they first entered the kingdom of King Eystein. But the leading men found out, and went to Uppsala and told King Eystein that a host had come into the land. The king had the war-arrow[32] sent throughout his kingdom, and summoned such a huge host that it was a wonder. Then he advanced his forces until he came to a forest, and he pitched his tents there. He now had the cow Sibilja with him, and she received many sacrifices before she was willing to travel.

When they were in the forest, King Eystein spoke. "I have found out", he said, "that Ragnar's sons are in the fields directly in front of the forest, and I have been told truly that they have not a third of the forces we have. Now we shall divide our ranks for the battle. One third of our men shall advance against them, and they are so bold that they will think that they have the business well in hand. Then we shall attack them with our full forces. And the cow will go in front of the army, and I expect that they shall not withstand her bellowing." And so it was done.

As soon as the brothers saw King Eystein's force, they thought that it wouldn't be too powerful to deal with, and they didn't suppose that his forces might be larger. Suddenly, all of his host came out of the forest. The cow was turned loose, and she charged in front of the ranks and bellowed horribly, and there was such great confusion among the fighters who heard it that they fought each other, except for the two brothers who managed to hold out. The evil creature gored many men with her horns that day. Though the sons of Ragnar were mighty, they could not withstand both such overwhelming forces and such sorcery, although they put up stiff resistance and defended themselves well, with bravery and great renown.

Eirek and Agnar were in the forefront of the ranks that day, and they often broke through the battle-lines of King Eystein. Then Agnar fell. Eirek saw that, and he bore himself more bravely than ever, and didn't care whether he survived or not—but he was surrounded by an overpowering force and captured.

Now Eystein said that the battle should stop, and he offered a truce to Eirek. "And I will grant you this as well," he said, "I will give you my daughter's hand in marriage." Eirek spoke a verse:

> I won't take my brother's blood-money,
> nor buy a maid with rings[33].
> It's now said that Eystein
> has become Agnar's bane.
> My mother won't mourn me;
> I'll mount up above the slain.
> Let the ravenous spear-shaft
> skewer me right through.

He said that he wanted the men who had followed him and Agnar to have safe conduct and to go wherever they wanted. "But I want as many spears as possible to be taken and to be stuck down in the ground, and there I will have myself lifted up on them, and there will I lay down my life." King Eystein said that what he had asked for would be done, although he had made the worst choice for both of them. Now the points of the spears were set down, and Eirek spoke a verse:

> No king's son shall ever—
> so I know my sentence—
> die on a dearer bed,
> a day's meal for the raven.
> The soot-black blood-seeker°   *blood-seeker*: raven
> will soon scream over the brothers,
> rip apart the pair of them,
> though it's a poor reward.

Now he went to the place where the spears were set down. He took a ring from his hand and threw it to those men who had followed him and had been given safe conduct. He dispatched them to Aslaug, and spoke a verse:

> Fare with my final words—
> finished are eastern journeys—
> the slender lady Aslaug
> may own my hoard of rings.
> There will be fiercest fury
> when they find out my death,
> if my stepmother speaks of it
> to her sons so gentle.

And now he was heaved up on the spears. Then he saw a raven flying, and he said to it:

> Now the slash-gull° soars high,   *slash-gull*: raven
> screaming over my head;
> the wound-falcon° wishes   *wound-falcon*: raven
> my warm, unseeing eyes.
> Know, if the bird should break
> the brow-stones° from my head,   *brow-stones*: eyes
> the raven pays me poorly
> for plenty of Ekkil's bounty°.   *Ekkil*: a sea-king; his *bounty*: corpses

Now he laid down his life with great courage.

But his messengers went home, and didn't stop until they came to where Ragnar had his royal seat. At the time, he had gone to a meeting of kings. Ragnar's sons had also not come home from raiding. The messengers were there for three nights before they went to meet Aslaug. When they came before Aslaug's high seat, they greeted her respectfully, and she began to speak with them. She had a linen kerchief on her knees and meant to comb her hair, and she had let her hair down. Now she asked who they were, for she had not seen them before. The one who spoke for them said that they had been warriors of Eirek and Agnar, Ragnar's sons. Then she spoke a verse:

> What tidings do you tell,
> trusted friend of kings?
> Are the Swedes assailing,
> or perhaps sent packing?
> I see that Danes have sailed
> from the south, northwards;
> the Hildings° had red rollers—   *Hildings*: princes
> I have no further knowledge.

He spoke a verse in reply:

> We must say to you, lady,
> what is sorely distressing—
> slain are the sons of Thora;
> sad the fates of your men.
> No other new tidings,
> we know, are heavy as these.
> I've come from hearing the news:
> over the corpse flies the eagle.

She asked what had happened. He spoke that verse which Eirek had spoken, when he sent the ring to her. They saw that she shed a tear: it looked like blood, and was as hard as a hailstone. No one had ever seen her shed a tear, neither before nor since.

Now she said that she could not plan vengeance before one or the other came home, Ragnar or his sons. "But you shall stay here till then. I will not fail to urge them to take revenge, just as if they were my own sons." And so they stayed there.

It so happened that Ivar and his brothers came home before Ragnar. They were not home long before Aslaug went to meet her sons. Sigurd was three years old at the time, and he went with his mother. And when she came into the hall where the brothers were having their discussion, they greeted her warmly. They asked for any other news, and they spoke about the fall of her son Rognvald, and about the events which had happened there. But that news didn't affect her much, and she said:

> My sons left me to stare
> at the seagull's land°, a long time;　　　　　　　　　*seagull's land:* sea
> you've been gadding about,
> going around begging.
> Rognvald soaked his shield
> in slain warriors' blood;
> he fared unafraid to Odin,
> of my fine sons the youngest.

"And I cannot see", she said, "how he could have lived for greater glory."

Now they asked what news she had. She answered, "The fall of Eirek and Agnar, your brothers and my stepsons, the men who were the best of warriors, as I believe. It will not be surprising if you refuse to tolerate such a thing, and exact terrible vengeance. I ask this of you, and I will assist you in everything, so that our revenge may be greater rather than less."

Ivar said, "This is certain: I will never come to Sweden for the purpose of fighting King Eystein and the sorcery that is there." She pressed him, but Ivar spoke for them all and completely refused to make the voyage. And now she spoke a verse:

> Had you been first to fall,
> without fail you would not
> be lying, lacking vengeance
> delayed for half a year,
> if Eirek and Agnar
> —I'll conceal it little—
> brethren not born of me,
> still did breathe and live.

"It's not certain", said Ivar, "whether that helps your case at all, though you speak one verse after another. How clearly do you know what sort of defenses we would be facing?"

"I don't know that certainly", she said. "What can you say about the obstacles there?"

Ivar said that there was such great sorcery, that no one said that he had ever heard that the like could exist. "And the king is both powerful and wicked."

"What does he worship most at sacrifice?"

He said, "It's a great cow, and she is called Sibilja. She has been made so powerful that as soon as men hear her bellowing, his enemies cannot withstand it. It is hardly as if we shall be battling with men alone; rather, I think that first we shall encounter sorcery, before we meet the king. I will not risk myself nor my men."

She said, "You might realize that you cannot be called the greatest of men if you don't strive for it."

Now that it seemed to her that it was in vain, she meant to leave; she thought that they didn't set much store by her words. Then Sigurd Snake-in-the-Eye spoke. "I must tell you, mother", he said, "what is in my mind, though I may not change their answers."

"I will listen to that", she said.

Now he spoke a verse:

> It will take us three nights,
> if you are troubled, mother—
> far must be our faring—
> for our forces to be ready.
> If blade-edges aid us, [34]
> Eystein the king shall not
> hold Uppsala's high seat,
> though hoarded wealth he offer.

When he had spoken this verse, the brothers' minds began to change somewhat. [35] Now Aslaug said, "Now you have made it known that you will do my will, my son. But I cannot see how we two will go on this journey, if we don't have help from your brothers. Yet it may turn out that this deed will be avenged, as seems best to me. I think it is good that you go, my son." And now Bjorn spoke a verse:

> A hawk-keen breast, holding
> bold heart and mind within,
> aids a man, though he make
> but little mention of it.
> Though no snakes nor serpents
> shimmer in our own eyes,
> my brothers made me merry,
> I remember your stepsons.

And now Hvitserk spoke a verse:

Let's plan before we promise,
plot to wreak our vengeance,
be blithe that Agnar's banesman
must bear a host of harms;
let's shove the boat off from shore,
shatter ice before the prow,
see how soon we can get
our sailing ships outfitted.

Hvitserk advised that they should break the ice because the river was hard frozen, and their ships were trapped in the ice. And now Ivar began to speak, and he said that things had come to the point that he must take part, and he spoke a verse:

You all boast of boundless
bravery and daring.
Now what you all need is
great tenacity as well.
I'll be hoisted above heroes,
because I have no bones, yet
I'll have a hand in vengeance,
whichever I make use of.[36]

"And now is the time", said Ivar, "for us to start planning, as best we can, to provision our ships and to summon a war-host, because we will need to leave nothing out, if we are to be victorious." Now Aslaug went away.

CHAPTER XI

Sigurd had had a foster-father, and he took care of both preparing the ships and getting men, so that they would all be ready. They worked so quickly that the force that Sigurd was in charge of was ready when three nights had passed; he had five ships, all well equipped. When five nights were past, Hvitserk and Bjorn had gotten fourteen ships ready. And when seven nights had passed from the time when they had made their plans and announced the voyage, Ivar had ten ships and Aslaug another ten.

Now they all met together, and each told the others how great a force he had raised. Ivar said that he had sent a force of knights by land. Aslaug said, "If I knew that that land force would be of use, then I might have sent a great host."

"We can't delay," said Ivar, "we must leave now, with such forces as we have drawn together."

Aslaug said that she would go with them —"and I know clearly what measures must be taken to avenge the brothers."

"This is certain", said Ivar, "you will not come on our ships. If you wish, you shall command the land forces." She said that it would be so. Now her name was changed, and she was called Randalin.[37]

Now both of the forces set out, and Ivar told the other force where they should meet. Both of them traveled well, and met at the place which had been agreed on. And where they landed in Sweden, in King Eystein's kingdom, they went harrying. They burned everything in front of them, killed every mother's son, and even more: they killed every living thing.

CHAPTER XII

It happened that some men escaped and found King Eystein. They told him that a great host had come to his kingdom, so hostile that they had left nothing undamaged: they had laid waste every place that they had passed through, and not a house was still standing. When King Eystein heard these tidings, he realized who these raiders must be. He had the war-arrow sent through all his kingdom, and summoned all his men who wanted to lend him their aid and who could bear shields. "We shall have with us the cow Sibilja, our god, and let her charge ahead of the host. I expect that it will go as before, that they will not be able to withstand her bellowing. I will encourage all my men to help as best they can, and we shall drive away this great and evil host."

It was done: Sibilja was let loose. Ivar saw her coming, and heard the savage bellowing coming from her. He ordered all his men to make a great uproar, clashing their weapons and shouting battle cries, so that they should hear as little as possible of the voice of this evil creature which came against them.

Ivar said to his bearers that they should carry him to the attack, as far forward as they could. "When that cow comes at us, throw me at her, and one of two things will happen: either I shall lay down my life, or else she will get her death. Now you must take a large tree and carve it into a bow shape, and arrows with it." Then he was brought the huge bow and the great arrows which he had ordered made, but no one thought that either would be useful as a weapon.

Now Ivar encouraged every man to help as best he could. His forces advanced, making a great noise, and Ivar was carried in front of their ranks. There was such a great noise when Sibilja bellowed that they heard it just as clearly as if they were silent and standing still. It frightened them so much that all the men wanted to fight each other, except for the brothers.

24

But when this terrible thing happened, Ivar's bearers saw that he drew his bow as if it were a flimsy elm twig. It seemed to them that he overdrew the arrows, with the points behind the bow. Now they heard his bowstring twang, so loudly that they had never heard it that way before. And they saw how his arrows flew as fast as if he had shot them from the strongest crossbow, and so straight that every arrow pierced Sibilja's eyes. She fell down and then tumbled head over heels, and her bellows became much worse than before. And when she came at them, he asked them to throw him at her—and he became as light to them as if they were throwing a little child, because they were not very close to the cow when they threw him. Then he landed on the back of the cow Sibilja, and he became as heavy as if a boulder had fallen on her. Every bone in her body was broken, and she died from this.

Now he ordered men to pick him up as soon as possible. When he was lifted up, his voice became so piercing that it seemed to all the fighters that he spoke as if he was next to them, although he was standing far away. He gave his orders in complete silence. And he ended his speech in this way: the hostility which was their reason for coming would be over soon, and nothing had hurt them, because their forces had fought for only a short time. Now Ivar encouraged them to do their worst to their enemies—"and now it seems that the most deadly one, that cow, is killed."

Both of the forces had formed up in ranks, and they went into battle. The fight was so fierce that all the Swedes said that they had never been in such a trial. The brothers Hvitserk and Bjorn advanced so fiercely that none of the ranks could withstand them. Now so many of King Eystein's forces fell that few were left standing, and some turned and fled. And so the battle ended: King Eystein fell, and the brothers won the victory. They granted a truce to the survivors.

Now Ivar said that he didn't want to harry any longer in that land, because that land was now leaderless. "And I would rather that we set sail to where a greater force is facing us." But Randalin went home with some of the men.

CHAPTER XIII

Now they made plans among themselves to raid in the southern realm. Sigurd Snake-in-the-Eye, Randalin's son, went with the brothers on every raiding journey. On this voyage they set a course for every sizable town and conquered it, so that none withstood them.

They heard about a certain town which was both large and populous, and strongly built. Ivar said that he wanted to head there. This is said about how the town was named, and who ruled it: the chieftain was called Vifil, and from his name the town was called Vifilsborg.[38] Now they harried so fiercely that they laid waste all the towns that they encountered, until they came to Vifilsborg. The chieftain was not at his home in his town, and many men had gone with him.

The brothers set up their tents on the plain which was next to the town. They were peaceful on the day when they came to the town, and they held a parley with the townsmen. They asked them whether they would rather give up the town, in which case peace would be granted to all, or whether they would take it by their overwhelming force and fierceness, and then no one would be offered a truce. But the townsmen dismissed them quickly, and said that they would never win that town by getting them to surrender it. "You must be first be tested, and show us your valor and eagerness."

Now the night passed. And the next day, they set out to conquer the town, and accomplished nothing. They surrounded the town for half a month and tried every day to conquer it, trying various strategies. But the longer they kept trying, the more distant the prospect seemed, and they intended to turn back. And when the townsmen became aware that they intended to turn back, they went out onto the town walls. They spread out bolts of costly fabric over all the walls, with all of the most beautiful clothes in the town, and over them they arranged gold and the greatest treasures of the town. Now one of their soldiers spoke up and said, "We thought that these men, the sons of Ragnar, and their followers were valiant men, but we can now say that they have done no better than the others." After that, they whooped at them and beat their shields and egged them on as much as they could.

When Ivar heard that, it greatly affected him. He got a great sickness from this, so that he could not move, and they had to wait for him to either get better or else perish. He lay all that day till evening, not speaking a word. Then he said to the men who were near him that they should tell Bjorn, Hvitserk and Sigurd that he wanted to meet with them and all the wisest men. And they all came to the same place, the greatest chieftains and their forces.

Ivar asked if they had come up with any plan that was more likely to succeed than the ones they had had before. They all answered that they didn't have the wit to come up with strategies that would win them victory. "But now, as often before, your plan will be useful."

Then Ivar answered, "One plan which we haven't tried has come into my mind. Here there is a great forest, not far away. When it becomes dark, we shall leave our tents and go to the forest, in secret—but our tents shall stay behind. When we come into the woods, every man shall tie up a bundle of sticks for himself. When that is done, we shall surround the town on all sides and set the wood on fire. A huge fire will be made, and their town walls will lose their mortar from the fire. We shall then bring up catapults and test how hardy the walls are."

And it was done: they went to the forest and stayed there for as long as Ivar thought fit. Then they went to the town according to his plan, and when they started a great fire with the wood, there was such a great blaze that the walls could not withstand it and lost their mortar. Then they brought catapults to the town and tore many gaps in the walls, and now the battle began. As soon as they faced each other in battle, the townsfolk's forces fell, but some fled. And so their dealings ended: they killed every man's child in the town and took all the wealth, but burned the town before they went away.

CHAPTER XIV

Now they set off from there, until they came to the town called Luna.[39] By then they had destroyed nearly every fort and every castle in all of the southern realms, and they were so famous in every household that there was not a child, no matter how little, who didn't know their names. They intended not to stop until they came to Rome, because that city was said to be both large and populous, and famous and wealthy. But they didn't know exactly how long a journey it was to there, and they had so many men that provisions couldn't be obtained.

They were in the town of Luna, discussing their journey among themselves. A man came up, old and good-natured. They asked what kind of a man he was. He said that he was a poor beggar and had traveled the land all his life.

"You must know many tidings to tell us, which we would like to know."

The old man answered, "I do not know any question that you might ask, about any land, which I don't know how to answer."

"What we want is for you to tell us how far the journey is from here to Rome."

He replied, "I can show you something as a sign. You see here these iron shoes which I have on my feet. They are now old, and these others that I carry on my back are now broken. But when I left Rome, I tied on my feet these broken ones which I now have on my back, and back then both pairs were new. I have been on that journey ever since."[40]

When the old man had said this, they realized that they could not go on the journey to Rome, as they had intended. Now they and their men turned back and conquered many towns that had never been taken before, and the signs of this may be seen to this day.

CHAPTER XV

Now we take up the story where Ragnar was staying at home in his kingdom, and he did not know where his sons were, nor Randalin, his wife. And he heard every one of his men say that no one was the equal of his sons, and it occurred to him that no one was as famous as they. Now he thought about how he might seek for fame that would be no less fleeting. He thought of a plan, and got himself shipwrights and had timber felled for two great ships. The people saw that they were two transports[41], so large that none like them had been made in the Northlands— and along with them, he ordered a great store of weapons from all his kingdom.

From these events, people found out that he meant to go on some war expedition of his own, away from his lands. The news was heard widely in those countries that were nearest. Now men and all the kings who ruled those lands feared that they might not be able to stay in their lands or kingdoms. Every one of them had a watch set on his land.

On one occasion, Randalin asked Ragnar what journey he was planning for himself. He told her that he intended to go to England, and to have no more ships than the two transports and the men that would fit in them. Randalin said, "This journey which you're proposing seems careless to me. I would think it advisable for you to have more ships and smaller ones."

"There's no glory in that," he said, "if men should conquer a land with many ships. But there are no old tales about how a land such as England was won with two ships. And if I am defeated, then the fewer ships I have taken away from my land, the better."

Randalin answered, "It seems no less expensive to me, instead of building these ships, for you to have many longships for this journey. But you know that it is bad for ships to sail for England. If it happens that your ship is wrecked, even if the men manage to come to land, they will have to surrender right away, if the lord of the land comes there. And it's better to steer longships into harbor than transports."

Now Ragnar spoke a verse:

> Let no man spare the Rhine's amber°   *Rhine's amber:* gold
> if he wants seasoned warriors;
> it's harmful for the helm-wise°   *helm-wise:* kings
> to hoard rings, rather than troops.
> It's hard to defend the fortress-gates
> with flame-red golden treasures;
> many kings have lost their lives,
> though their riches live on after.

He had his ships loaded and got himself a host of men, so that the transports were fully loaded. Now his intentions were clear. And then he spoke a verse:

What does the ring-breaker° hear

ring-breaker: king

come from the rocks howling,

that the flinger of hand-fire°

hand-fire: gold; its *flinger:* king

must forsake his fleet sea-serpents?°

sea-serpents: ships

Yet I, who freely scatter

all the forearm's layings°,

forearm's layings: gold arm-rings

shall bear with this plan bravely,

brooch-Bil°, if the gods will.

Bil: moon-goddess; *brooch-Bil:* woman

When his ships were made ready, along with the host that should go with him, and then when a wind came that seemed favorable, Ragnar said that he had to go to the ships. And when he was ready, he led her to the ships. Before they parted, she said that she would reward him for the shirt which he had given to her. He asked how she would do it. She spoke this verse:

Stitched and seamed nowhere,
this long shirt I give you;
out of hoar-grey hair-strands,
with a high heart, I wove it.
No wound will be bloody,
nor will weapons bite you
if you have this hallowed tunic,
made holy by the gods.

He said that he would accept this advice. And when they parted, it was clear that she was deeply moved by their parting.

Now Ragnar steered his ships to England, as he had planned. He encountered rough weather, so that he wrecked both of his ships on the coast of England, but all his forces came to land, and they held on to their clothing and weapons. And where he came upon villages and towns and castles, he took them.

The king who ruled over England was named Ælle.[42] He had received news that Ragnar had left his own country. He had set men to keep watch so that he might know immediately if the host attacked his land. Now men went to meet with King Ælle and tell him the news of war. He had a summons sent throughout all his kingdom and called on every man who could wield a shield and ride a horse, and who dared to fight, to come to him. He got together such a great host that it was a wonder. King Ælle prepared himself for battle. Then he said to his men, "If we gain the victory in this battle, and if you become aware that Ragnar has come, then you must not raise a weapon against him, because he has left sons behind, who will never leave us alone if he falls."

Ragnar now prepared himself for battle. He had the shirt that Randalin had given him at their parting, worn over his mail coat. And he had in his hand the spear with which he had vanquished the serpent which lay around Thora's hall, which no one else had dared. He had no other protection, except for a helm.

And where they met, the battle began. Ragnar had much smaller forces. The battle had not gone on long before many of Ragnar's men fell. But wherever he went, the host fell back before him. He broke through the ranks that day, and wherever he hewed or struck shields, mail or helms, his blows were so strong that no one withstood them. But he was never struck or shot; not one weapon did him harm, and he never received a wound, but he killed a great many of King Ælle's men. Yet the battle ended in this way: all of Ragnar's forces were killed, and he was pressed down with shields and so taken prisoner. Now he was asked who he was, but he was silent and didn't answer. Then King Ælle said, "This man must be put through a greater trial, if he will not tell us who he is. I will cast him in an enclosure of serpents and let him sit there for a very long time. If he says anything by which we may discern that he is Ragnar, he will be taken out as fast as possible."

This was done to him straightaway. He sat there for a very long time, such that the snakes never fastened themselves onto him. The men said, "This man is mighty; no weapons bit him all day, and now none of the snakes will hurt him."

King Ælle said that he was to be stripped of the clothes that he had outermost, and it was done, and the snakes hung onto him with all their might. Then Ragnar said, "The piglets would grunt now, if they knew what the old pig suffers." And though he spoke in this way, they didn't clearly realize that it was Ragnar, rather than another king. Now he spoke a verse:

> I have fought 'gainst foes in
> fifty-one battles in all,
> which seemed a splendid feat,
> I did scathe to many men;
> I never imagined a snake
> for the ending of my life;
> many things may happen
> which men themselves expect least.

And he spoke again:

> The piglets would protest loudly
> if the boar's plight they knew.

Death has been dealt to me,
snakes dig in my flesh-house
and savagely stab me,
serpents suck my life out.
beside the beasts I'll die now,
soon I will be a corpse.

Then he laid down his life, and he was carried out of there.

King Ælle realized that Ragnar had died. Now he thought about himself—how he should take precautions or manage affairs so that he might hold onto his kingdom, or find out how it would affect Ragnar's sons when they heard of it. He hit upon a plan: he had a ship readied, and got a man to carry out his plan who was both wise and hardy, and he got men so that the ship was well crewed. He said that he wanted to send them to meet Ivar and the brothers and tell them of the fall of their father. But the trip seemed most unlikely to succeed, so that few wanted to go.

Then the king said, "On this mission you must carefully observe how each of the brothers reacts to this news. Set your course as soon as you get fair winds." He had provided for their journey, so that they needed nothing else. And now they left, and their journey went well.

The sons of Ragnar had raided in the southern realms. Then they turned back to the Northlands, and intended to visit the kingdoms that Ragnar ruled. But they didn't know how his war-journey had gone, though they were very curious about how it had turned out. They came up from the southern lands. Everywhere that men heard that the brothers were coming, they feared for their towns and fled, carrying their wealth away, so that the brothers' forces hardly got any food.

One morning, Bjorn Ironsides awoke and spoke a verse:

Here flies each fair morning,
over these fortresses,
the hale hawk-of-the-slain°—   *hawk of the slain:* raven
he'll die hungry, without luck.
He should go south o'er sands,
where sore wounds we have made,
drink the gore of dead men,
dew that wells from axe-cuts.

And he also said:

When we reived in the realm
of the Roman kingdom,

31

I first took up Frey's game°,
where fighters were well matched;
there I showed my sword—
eagle screamed over corpses—
for the murderous man-scathe
of the gray-mustached ones.

Frey's game: battle

CHAPTER XVI

Now it happened that Ragnar's sons came to Denmark before the messengers of King Ælle, and they stayed there quietly with their men. But the messengers came with their troops to the town where the sons of Ragnar were being feasted, and went into the hall where they drank, and stood before the high seat where Ivar lay. Sigurd Snake-in-the-Eye and Hvitserk the Swift sat playing a board game[43], but Bjorn Ironsides was planing a spear-shaft on the hall floor.

When the messengers of King Ælle came before Ivar, they addressed him respectfully. But he began to question them, asking where they were from and what news they would tell. Their leader said that they were Englishmen, and King Ælle had sent them there to tell the news of the fall of Ragnar, their father. Hvitserk and Sigurd dropped their game pieces, and carefully observed the report of this news. Bjorn stood up on the hall floor and propped himself up with his spearshaft. But Ivar asked them carefully about every detail of his death. They told everything that had happened, from the time that he invaded England, to the time that he laid his life down. When the story came to the point where he had said "The piglets would grunt," Bjorn clenched his hand on the spear-shaft, and he gripped it so hard that his handprint could be seen later.

When the messengers finished their story, Bjorn shook the spearpoint apart, so that it split into two pieces. Hvitserk gripped a game piece which he had captured, and he squeezed it so hard that blood spurted out from under every nail. Sigurd Snake-in-the-Eye had held a knife and was paring down his nails when these tidings were told, and he pondered the news so deeply that he didn't realize that the knife was sticking in the bone—and he didn't flinch. But Ivar asked for every last detail, and his complexion turned red for a while, then black for a while, and periodically went pale. He was so enraged that his skin was all swollen from the savagery in his breast.

Hvitserk began to speak, and he said that they might get their revenge most quickly by killing King Ælle's messengers.

Ivar said, "That must not happen. They shall go in peace wherever they wish, and if there is anything that they are short of, they may tell me and I shall get it for them."

Now that the messengers had finished their errand, they turned and walked out of the hall and went to their ships. When they got a favorable wind, they sailed out to sea and traveled well until they came to meet with King Ælle. They told him how each one of the brothers had reacted to the news. When King Ælle heard that, he said to them, "This is to be expected: either we must fear Ivar, or no one, because of what you say about him. The other brothers will be mild-hearted, and we can hold our kingdom against them." Now he had a watch set over all his kingdom, so that no invaders might catch him unawares.

When the messengers of King Ælle had gone away, the brothers held a council, concerning how they should proceed to avenge Ragnar, their father. Ivar said, "I will not take part, and I will not summon my men, because Ragnar did just as I was afraid he would. He handled this matter badly from the beginning. He had no quarrel with King Ælle, and it has often happened that if a man unjustly plans aggression, he is laid low in dishonor. I will accept monetary compensation from King Ælle, if he will grant it to me."

But when his brothers heard that, they became very angry and said that they should never be such cowards, even if he wanted it so. "Many will say that we have wrongly given our allegiance[44] if we fail to avenge our father, though we have gone raiding far from home and killed many innocent men. That shall not happen. Rather, we must prepare every ship in Denmark that is seaworthy. We shall summon all our forces together, so that every man who can bear a shield against King Ælle must go."

But Ivar said that he would leave his ships behind, "except for the one which I have myself." And when it was heard that Ivar would take no part in this, they got a much smaller host, and yet they went nonetheless.

When they had come to England, King Ælle found out. At once he had his trumpets sounded, and summoned to himself all the men who would follow him. He assembled such a great host that no man could count them, and went out against the brothers. When they encountered each other, Ivar was not in the battle. And the battle ended thus: Ragnar's sons turned and fled, and King Ælle won the victory.

As Ælle was pursuing the fleeing host, Ivar said that he intended not to return to his own land—"and I will find out whether King Ælle will grant me some honors or not. It seems better to me to accept compensation than to go on any more unlucky voyages, such as we have now gone on."

Hvitserk said that he would have no part in this with him, and that he could go about his business as he wanted—"but we shall never accept money for our father."

Ivar said that he would part with them there, and asked them to rule the kingdom which they all had in common—"but you must send me money when I request it."

When he had spoken, he bid them farewell. He turned back to meet King Ælle. When he had come before him, he addressed the king respectfully and began to state his case: "I have come to meet you, and I wish to discuss making peace with you, and talk about such honors as you will have done for me. I now see that I have nothing against you, and it seems better to me to receive from you such honors as you will grant me, than to surrender my men to you, or myself."

King Ælle answered, "Some men say that it is not easy to trust you; you often speak fair to them, when you think falsely. It will be difficult for us to keep an eye on you or your brothers."

"I will ask for little from you, if you will grant it. And I shall swear to you that I shall never oppose you."

Now the king asked about what he had said about compensation. "I want", said Ivar, "for you to give me as much of your land as an ox-hide will span, and around that, I shall build a foundation. I will not ask any more of you than this. And this I know: you won't do me any honor if you're not willing to do this."

"I don't know", said the king, "how it could do us any harm if you have this piece of my land. Certainly I will give you that, if you will swear not to fight against me. I do not fear your brothers, if you are true to me."

CHAPTER XVII

They discussed the matter between themselves, and Ivar swore an oath to King Ælle that he would not launch an attack against him and not devise plots to harm him, and he should own as much of England as could be spanned by the largest ox-hide he could get.

Now Ivar got the hide of an old bull and had it softened, and he had it stretched three times. Then he had it cut apart as thinly as possible, and then he had the hairy side split from the flesh side. When this was done, that thong was so long that people marveled at it; it hadn't occurred to anyone that it might become so long. Then he had it stretched out in a field, and it encircled a plot of land so wide that it was the size of a large town. On the outside, he had the foundations marked for a great city wall. Then he got many carpenters and had many houses raised on that field, and there he had a great city built, called London Town.[45] It is the largest and most famous of all towns in all the Northlands.

Now that he had this town built, he gave away treasure, and he was so generous that he gave with both hands. He seemed so great in wisdom that everyone sought him for advice in difficult cases, and he settled all cases in such a way that each party thought that he came out on top. He made so many friends that he had friendship with every man. King Ælle had much help from him in ruling the land, so that the king had him look after many of his affairs and cases, and didn't have to deal with them himself.

When Ivar had proceeded so far with his plans that his intentions seemed completely peaceful to everyone, he sent men to meet with his brothers, with a request to send him as much gold and silver as he asked for. And when these men came to meet the brothers, they spoke their message, and told how his plan was coming along—because no one could figure out what sort of strategy he was plotting. The brothers realized that he wasn't in his customary state of mind. They sent as much money as he had asked for.

When the messengers came to Ivar, he gave all his money to the most important men in the land, and so he lured away King Ælle's fighing men: they all swore that they would stay home peacefully, even if Ælle might go to war later. And when Ivar had drawn up this force under his command, he sent men to meet with his brothers and tell them that he wanted them to raise the levy from all the lands that they ruled, and summon every man that they had. When this message came to the brothers, they quickly realized that Ivar thought that now they had their best chances of gaining a victory. They summoned their men from all of Denmark and Gotland and all the kingdoms that they ruled, and got an overwhelming force together and assembled their levy outdoors. Then they set their ships' courses for England, sailing both by night and by day, for they wanted as little news of their coming as possible to go before them.

King Ælle was told the news of war. He summoned his men but got few, because Ivar had drawn a great many men out from under him. Now Ivar went to meet King Ælle and said that he would fulfill the oath that he had sworn: "I cannot change my brothers' plans, but I can try to meet them and find out whether they will halt their forces and do no more harm than they have already done."

Ivar went to meet his brothers, and he strongly encouraged them to advance as quickly as they could and hold the battle as soon as possible, "because the king has a much smaller force." They answered that he didn't need to encourage them, and that they were in the same mood as before.

Now Ivar went to meet with King Ælle, and told him that they were much too eager to fight and too furious to want to listen to his words. "And when I tried to reach a truce between you and them, they howled in reply. Now I must fulfill my oath that I will not fight against you. I and my men will peacefully stay nearby, but the battle will go with you however it may turn out."

King Ælle saw the brothers' forces, and they advanced with such fury that it was a wonder. Then Ivar said "Now it's time, King Ælle, for you to deploy your forces, and I guess that they will attack you fiercely for a while." And where the armies met each other, there was a great battle, and the sons of Ragnar charged right through King Ælle's ranks. They were so enraged that they only thought of doing as much damage as possible, and the battle was both long and hard. And in the end, King Ælle and his forces turned and fled, and he was taken prisoner.

Ivar was nearby, and he said that they should now bring about his death. "My advice now", he said, "is that we remember the sort of death that he ordered for our father. Now the man who is the most skilled woodcarver shall carve an eagle on his back as carefully as possible, and that eagle shall turn red with his blood."[46]

The man who was summoned for this task did as Ivar asked him, and King Ælle was terribly wounded before the task was completed. He now lay down his life, and it seemed to the brothers that they had avenged their father Ragnar. Ivar said that he would give them the kingdom that they had all ruled together, but he wanted to rule over England.

CHAPTER XVIII

After that, Hvitserk and Bjorn went home to their own kingdoms, and Sigurd as well, but Ivar stayed behind and ruled England. From then on, they joined their forces together less often, and raided in various lands.

Randalin, their mother, was an old woman by then. Hvitserk, her son, had gone raiding on a certain occasion in the eastern realms, and such overwhelming forces came against him that he could not withstand them, and he was taken prisoner. But he chose his own death-day: they were to make a pyre out of men's heads, and there he would burn. In this way he laid down his life.[47] And when Randalin heard that, then she spoke this verse:

One son whom I suckled
sought death in the East-realm,
Hvitserk he was named,
never hurrying to flee;
they heated him with hacked-off
heads of the slain in battle;
my bold and brave prince chose
this bane, before he died.

And then she said:

They ordered countless heads
heaped beneath the warrior,
so the flame would keen the dirge
over the doomed folk-tree.°   *folk-tree*: king
What better bed should a battle-oak°   *battle-oak*: warrior
spread beneath himself?
The powerful one dies proudly—
the prince chose this fall.

A great lineage is descended from Sigurd Snake-in-the-Eye. His daughter was named Ragnhild, the mother of Harald Fairhair, the first sole ruler of all Norway.

Ivar ruled all England till his dying day, and he died of a sickness. As he was lying on his deathbed, he said that they should carry him to the place where invaders might come, and he said that he expected that they would not get victory when they landed. When he had breathed his last, it was done as he had requested, and a howe was raised. And many men say that when King Harald Sigurdarson[48] came to England, he came to the spot where Ivar had been laid before, and he fell on that journey. But when William the Bastard[49] landed, he went to Ivar's howe and tore it down, and he found that Ivar was undecayed. Then he had a great pyre made, and had Ivar burned on the pyre, and after that he fought for the land and won a victory.[50]

Many people are descended from Bjorn Ironsides. From him is descended a great lineage: Thord, who lived at Hofud in Hofdastrond, a great chieftain.[51]

And when the sons of Ragnar had all died, their men dispersed along the various paths which they had followed. It seemed to all of them who had been with Ragnar's sons that there was no worth in any other chieftain. There were two men who traveled widely through the land to see if they could find any chieftain who seemed to be no disgrace to serve, but they didn't travel together.

CHAPTER XIX

It so happened in a distant land that a certain king had two sons. He became ill and expired, and his sons wanted to hold a funeral feast in his honor. They invited everyone who heard this news over the next three years to come to the feast. The news was heard far and wide throughout the land. For three years they prepared for this feast.

When that summer came, and the appointed time came for the drinking of the inheritance ale[52], there was such a great multitude of men that no one could tell how many there were. There were many great halls fitted out, and many tents outside.

And when the first evening had mostly passed, one man came to these halls. This man was so large that no one there was as large. They saw from his dress that he was a man of high birth. When he came into the hall, he went before the brothers and greeted them, and asked where they meant for him to sit. They were well pleased with him and told him to sit at the highest bench. He took up enough space for two men. And as soon as he had sat down, he was brought drink like the other men, and no horn was so large that he couldn't drink it down in one draught. It seemed to everyone that he thought there was no worth in any of the others.

Then it happened that another man came to this feast. He was even larger than the first man. These men had long hoods. And when this man came before the high seat of the young kings, he addressed them elegantly and asked them to direct him to a seat. They said that this man should sit closer in on the upper bench. Now he took his seat, and together they both were so large that five men had to stand up to give them room. But the one who arrived first was the lesser man at drinking; the second one drank so swiftly that he nearly guzzled every horn, and yet men couldn't tell that he was drunk. He behaved rather disagreeably to his benchmates and turned his back on them.

The one who had come first asked that they should have a game together—"and I will go first." He thrust out his hand towards the second man and spoke a verse:

> Speak to us of your honor,
> let's settle this, I ask you:
> have you seen the raven shiver,
> sated with blood, on its perch?
> More often you sat at feasts,
> sprawled upon the high-seat,
> than you carved bloody carrion
> for corpse-birds° in the valley.

corpse-birds: ravens

Now it seemed to the one who sat on the outside, that the one who had addressed him had challenged him, and he spoke a verse in response:

> Be silent, you sluggard!
> Shabby wretch, what have you done?
> You have dared no deeds that
> outdo my own glory;
> you didn't sate the sun-seeker,° [53]
> the bitch, at the sword's game°;
> you refused to give gore
> to the giantess's steed.°

sun-seeking bitch: wolf

sword's game: battle

giantess's steed: wolf

Now the one who had arrived first answered:

> We pushed the sea-prancer's°　　　　　　　　　　*sea-prancer:* ship
> strong prow through the surf
> as bright byrnies' sides
> with blood were spattered;
> the she-wolf was slavering
> as we sated eagles' hunger
> with red gore from men's gullets,
> winning grain of the fishes' heath°.　　*fishes' heath:* seafloor; its *grain:* gold

And now the one who had come second spoke:

> You never were found foremost,
> when Heiti's field° we saw,　　　　　*Heiti:* a sea-king; his *field:* sea
> spread before the white steeds
> of seagulls' wide journeys.°　　*seagulls' journeys:* sea; its *steeds:* ships
> Against the latch you trembled
> before we turned to the land,
> brought the red prows around
> towards the raven's kingdom.°　　　　　*raven's kingdom:* land

The one who had come first spoke:

> It's not fitting to fight over
> the foremost seat at banquets
> over glory we've each gained
> that's greater than the other's.
> You stood there, as swells bore
> the sword-hart° through the sound;　　　　　*sword-hart:* ship
> I rested there, as the red prow
> rode into safe harbor.

Now the one who had come second answered:

> Bjorn we both once followed
> into every blades' clash,
> firm and faithful champions
> when we fought for Ragnar;

39

when the brave did battle
in the Bulgars' kingdom,
I suffered a wound in the side—
now sit by me, neighbor!

And they recognized each other at last, and stayed at the feast.

CHAPTER XX

There was a man named Ogmund, who was called Ogmund the Dane. He once traveled with five ships and anchored on the coast of Samsø, in Munar Bay. It is said that his cooks went on land to get provisions, but his other men went into the forest to amuse themselves. There they found an ancient wooden man, forty ells high and overgrown with moss, yet all his features were visible. They discussed among themselves who must have sacrificed to this huge god. And then the wooden man spoke:

So long ago,
the sons of Haekling
rode this way
in roller-warships,
sailing the salt trail
of the sea-trout°.   *trail of the sea-trout*: sea
Then I was chosen
as chief of this village.[54]

Southward by the sea,
I was set up
by the shining-sworded
sons of Lodbrok;
they sacrificed to me
for the slaying of men
in the southern part
of Samsø.

There they said I should stay
while the shore lasts,
a man next to thorns,
moss-overgrown.

Now the clouds
cast tears on me;
neither covers me,
not clothes nor flesh.

This seemed extraordinary to the men, and they told it to others.

SÖGUBROT

The beginning and end of the Sögubrot *manuscript are illegible, and the middle two pages are also missing. Fortunately, enough information is preserved in other texts to make the story comprehensible.*

According to Ynglinga saga, *the legendary king Halfdan the Valiant had a son named Ivar. Halfdan's brother was Gudrod, the king of Skåne—the southern tip of the modern nation of Sweden, but at the time separate from the kingdom of the Swedes, which was centered on Uppsala to the northeast.* Ynglinga saga *also tells about King Ingjald of Sweden, who had enlarged his kingdom by killing twelve other kings through foul means, earning the name of* Ingjald illráða, *"Bad Ruler". His daughter Asa married Gudrod, somehow forced Gudrod to kill his own brother Halfdan, and then arranged for Gudrod to be killed in turn.*

To avenge his father and uncle, Ivar invaded Ingjald's kingdom. Outnumbered and surrounded, Ingjald and Asa got themselves and their entire retinue dead drunk, and then burned down their own hall. Then Ivar took the whole of Sweden. Ynglinga saga *adds that Ivar also took Denmark, and went on to conquer lands from northern England all the way to Russia. For this he was known as* Ívarr inn víðfaðmi, *"Ivar the Widely Embracing", or "Ivar Wide-Grasp".*

The Sögubrot *begins by telling how Ivar took Denmark. The hero Helgi the Keen, king at Zealand, has come to Ivar to ask for the hand of his daughter, Aud the Deep-Minded.[1] But Ivar has evidently learned a trick or two from Ingjald and Asa. . .*

CHAPTER I

. . . to refuse. The king answered, "I see that in this case, it's necessary not to spread it around that men are asking for your hand, for it was formerly the way of kings' daughters to let three suitors or more come, and not take the first. There are many kings that are better bred than Helgi."

Aud[2] replied, "It doesn't matter much whether or not you ask me about this, because I know that you've already made up your mind that things won't go the way I want them to. It's not likely that you will make such a good match for me. You must have something else in mind for me."

The king stood up and answered, "You've guessed rightly. You'll never get King Helgi, and the more you yearn for him, the less likely that will be."

He now met with King Helgi and said to him that he had advised in the matter on behalf of his daughter, and he said that he had acted with the utmost discretion, but her answers seemed foolish, notwithstanding all the time they'd discussed it. He said that there was no king's son who seemed to her to be a worthy match, so very great had her insolence grown. Nonetheless, he allowed again that he would discuss the matter at hand—"but as matters stand, it's no use."

Helgi went home, and Hraerek, his brother, heard about it. As he stayed at home in the kingdom, Hraerek's friends urged him to marry. That suited his mind well, and they advised that he should ask for the daughter of King Ivar, who was the most famous king at the time. He thought it unlikely that he would get her hand, for his brother didn't get it, who was much more prominent in every respect. They said that he would not get that match if he didn't ask, and said it would be no disgrace to him, even if the woman should turn him down. Then he brought up the matter before his brother and asked him to advise. Helgi said that it was an excellent idea, if he could get her. He also said that he didn't know who would get her, but that whoever won her would be lucky.

Now Hraerek asked Helgi to go and ask for the woman for him. Helgi said that he would go, but he expected that it wouldn't do any good, just as before. Helgi went to Sweden to meet King Ivar, and he was welcomed there, as before. He had been there a short time before he brought up the matter, and now he asked for Aud on behalf of his brother.

The king answered glumly and said that his request was unwise. He said that there wasn't hope—"and I wonder why you came with this request. If she didn't find it suitable to go with you, then why would she want someone who is much less prominent?"

Helgi said that Hraerek was no less worthy than himself in any way, but he wasn't equally famous—the reason was that he was always at home in the kingdom, and therefore less was said about him. He asked him to bring the case before Aud. The king said that he was reluctant, and told him to expect a bad answer from her, as before.

The next day, he called his daughter to him for a private meeting, and said that King Helgi had come and asked for her on behalf of his brother—"and he wants to know your answer to this request."

She answered that this time it must not turn out as it did before. She would not do such disrespect to Helgi's journey that she would welcome an offer for her to be given to Hraerek.

The king answered, "Your answer is worthless to me. I don't know how you think you'll get a husband if you refuse the offer of every king who asks for you. I think that you will quickly become unmanageable, if you won't take our advice."

She answered, "Talking about this with me won't change anything now, just as before. You must already have determined what match I must have. Whether I am given to Hraerek, or another man, doesn't change the fact that I will have a bad match made for me, at your hands."

The king went away and met with Helgi. He asked how his mission would go from then on. The king answered that she was very taken with him. "Word has it that my daughter is the wisest of women, but she would be the greatest fool, if she would not choose any other course than to deny you, such a king as you are. I esteem you far more highly than Hraerek. It seems most likely to me that she will have what she has requested for herself."

And thus they concluded their arrangement: he promised his daughter to Hraerek. Now she was made ready for the journey with Helgi. They went on their way, and when they left the Swedish realm, they discussed between themselves how the matter had gone and what king Ivar had planned for each of them. They now came home to the kingdom of Zealand. Hraerek heard of their coming, and had riding horses and a great escort sent to meet them. He ordered a feast to be prepared, and at that feast he took Aud as his wife. Helgi stayed at home on Zealand that winter, and that summer he went raiding, as was his custom.

Hraerek had a son by his wife, and he was named Harald.[3] This mark was on him: there were teeth in the front of his head, and they were large and golden in color.[4] He was tall and handsome in appearance, and when he was three years old, he was as large as a ten-year-old boy.

CHAPTER II

One summer, King Ivar came with his host from the east, from Sweden to Jutland. He sailed with all his forces to Zealand. He sent word to Hraerek, his son-in-law, that he should come to see him. The king told Aud, his wife. She asked whether he intended to go to meet his father-in-law to invite him to a feast on land. And in the evening, when King Hraerek went to sleep, Aud had ordered a new bed with all the bedclothes to be prepared, and it was set in the middle of the floor. She asked the king to sleep there and to remember what he dreamed—"and tell me in the morning". She took a different bed for herself.[5]

In the morning, Aud came and asked about his dream. "I dreamed", he said, "that I was near a certain forest, next to a beautiful even meadow. I saw a hart standing there in the meadow. Then a leopard ran out of the forest, and its mane looked like gold to me. The hart stuck its horns under the shoulder of the beast, and it fell down dead. Then next I saw how a great winged dragon flew to where the hart was, and gripped it in its claws and tore it apart. Then I saw a bear, and a young cub followed it. The dragon wanted to take the cub, but the bear protected it—and then I awoke."

She said, "That is an important dream. You should beware of King Ivar, my father, lest he deceive you when you meet him, because you have seen the fetches[6] of kings, and they will meet each other in battle. It would be better if you didn't have the hart which appeared to you, but that's what seems likeliest to me."

That same day, Hraerek traveled with many men to meet King Ivar, and went on the king's ship, in front of the afterdeck, and greeted King Ivar. But he didn't answer, and behaved as if he didn't see him. Then Hraerek said that he had a feast prepared to welcome him, and he wished to invite him to his own house. The king answered and said that he had made a poor match for his daughter, and said that it was no wonder, since she had treated him so badly. Hraerek answered that he was happy with their relationship, and said that he supposed that she was not displeased with it.

Then the king answered angrily, and said that Hraerek didn't clearly understand how Helgi and Aud were treating him. He said that it was on every man's lips that Harald was the son of King Helgi, and the boy looked just like him. And he said that he had come to let him know of this betrayal, and he said that it was evident to him that they could not both be married to her—"and I'd rather you give her to your brother than you go on this way any longer, not daring to take revenge."

Hraerek pretended that he had not heard that. But above all else, he didn't want to leave his wife, and he asked King Ivar to give him advice. Ivar said that he didn't know anything definite to tell him, other than that he should kill Helgi, and he declared that things never would be right with them, unless he gave up his wife to Helgi. He said that the situation was unbearable. Hraerek said that he would never let his wife go, and rather would take vengeance. He rode away with his men, but the king went south to Jutland.

In the autumn, when Helgi came home, Hraerek was so upset that no one could get a word out of him. But Aud had a grand feast prepared to greet him, and at that feast there were many kinds of games. It seemed to Helgi to be a great pity that his brother was so gloomy, and he asked him to enter a contest with him, but Hraerek said that he wouldn't play at present. Helgi asked him to be cheerful —"and we'll take our horses and have a jousting tournament, the way that we usually do."

Hraerek sprang up, went to his men without speaking, took up his weapons— helm and mailcoat and sword and spear—and rode out. The other men jousted with blunt lances. Helgi, his brother, rode at him with a lance. Hraerek thrust under Helgi's arm with the spear and ran him through, and he fell from the horse, dead. Now everyone who was nearby rode up to him and asked why he had done this evil thing. He declared that he had sufficient reason for it, and said that he had found out the truth that Helgi had led his wife astray. Everyone denied this and said that it was a great lie.

And when Aud heard that, she realized that that was her father's plan, "and yet not everything has happened as he planned," as she said would soon be evident. She took her son, Harald, and rode away with many men, but Hraerek went on his round of feasts,[7] as was his custom.

A little while later, King Ivar came from the south. When Hraerek heard that, he rode to meet him. And when King Ivar heard that Helgi had been killed, he said that this was a most dastardly deed, and he ordered his men to arm themselves quickly and avenge his friend Helgi. He heard that Hraerek intended to meet him, and he prepared his forces for an attack. They went up onto the land and into the forest where the road was which he knew that Hraerek would take. Hraerek came down to the sea, and King Ivar went ashore himself with the force that was left behind by the ships, and he had his banner raised and advanced against Hraerek. When the men in the forest heard King Ivar's trumpets, they ran out of the forest in pursuit of Hraerek and his forces. And when they encountered each other, they fought. Hraerek fell there, and all his men. Then King Ivar commanded that that kingdom be given to him in stewardship, and all those who were nearest went under his rule.

A little later, Aud the Deep-Minded, his daughter, came down from the land with all the forces that she had gotten together. Because King Ivar didn't have a large enough force to fight the people of the land at the time, he left and returned to Sweden.

That same winter, Aud got together all the gold and treasures that she could get in the kingdom that King Hraerek had ruled, and sent them to Gotland. And as soon as spring came, she made ready for her journey. She had Harald, her son, with her. Many important men left the land with her, and she had with her all the money that she could carry. She went first to Gotland and then east to Russia[8]. A king named Radbard ruled there. He welcomed her and her men, and invited her and all her men to stay with him and be highly honored in his land. She accepted.

King Ivar laid under his own rule all that the brothers had had.

King Radbard asked Aud to marry him. Because she was exiled from Zealand with her son, it seemed to her that she needed some support which could help her son when he grew up. Because Radbard was a powerful king, she was married to him according to Harald's advice—but King Ivar was not told.

CHAPTER III

When King Ivar heard the news that Aud was married, it seemed to him that

King Radbard was incredibly rash to take her without his leave. He gathered a great host from his entire kingdom, from Sweden and Denmark—such a great host that he could not tell how many ships he had. He set off with his forces to the eastern realm to capture King Radbard, and ordered them to devastate and burn all his kingdom. King Ivar was very old by then. And when he brought his forces eastwards to the Bay of Karelia[9], intending to disembark from the ships with his host, that was where King Radbard's kingdom began.

Then one night, as the king slept on the aft deck[10] of his flagship, it seemed to him that a great dragon flew out from the sea, and his appearance seemed to be all golden. Glowing cinders flew from him up to the heavens, like sparks fly out of a forge, and lit up all the lands around him. And after him flew all of the birds that there were in the Northlands, or so it seemed to him. Then he looked in another direction and saw that a great cloud came up from the northeast, and there followed such torrents and gusts, that it seemed as though all the forests and all the land would be washed away in the water as it rained down. Thunder and lightning followed. And when he saw the great dragon fly from the seas to the land, there came against him the rain and the storm wind and such a great darkness, that in a moment he could not see the dragon nor the birds, though he heard the great din of the thunders and the gales, and so they all passed south and west over the land, as widely as his kingdom reached. And then he seemed to look towards where the ships were, and they had all turned completely into whales, and swam out to sea.

Then he woke up, and he had Hord, his foster-father, summoned. He told him the dream and asked him to interpret it. Hord said that he was so very aged that he didn't know how to make any sense of dreams. He stood on a rock down off the head of the pier, and the king lay on the after-deck and loosened the long edges of his tent so that they could converse.

The king was not in good spirits and said, "Come on board the ship, Hord, and interpret my dream."

Hord said that he would not come aboard—"and your dream needs no interpretation. You yourself can understand what it is: more than likely, in only a little while, the rulership of Sweden and Denmark will change. Now the Hel-greed has come upon you, so that you think that all kingdoms must lie under your rule. But you don't realize that it will come to pass that you'll be dead, and your enemies will seize the kingdom."

The king said, "Come here and speak your wicked prophecies."

Hord said "Here will I stand and speak them from here."

The king said, "Who was Halfdan the Valiant among the Æsir?"

Hord said, "He was Balder among the Æsir, whom all the gods mourned, and not like you."

49

"You speak well," said the king, "Come here and tell your tidings."

Hord said "Here will I stand and speak them from here."

The king inquired, "Who was Hrærek among the Æsir?"

Hord said, "He was Hoenir, the most timid of the Æsir, and yet bad to you."

"Who was Helgi the Keen among the Æsir?" said the king.

Hord said, "He was Hermod, the best of the brave, and not useful to you."

The king said, "Who was Gudrod among the Æsir?"

Hord said, "Heimdall he was, the dullest[11] of all the Æsir, and yet bad to you."

The king said, "Who am I among the Æsir?"

Hord said, "You must be that serpent that is the worst of all, called the Midgard Serpent."

The king replied, very angry, "If you're telling me that I am doomed to die, then I tell you that you will not live long, for I recognize you where you stand, you great ogre. Come close to the Midgard Serpent, and we two will fight each other."

Then the king leaped from the afterdeck, and he was so angry that he leaped out from under the edges of his tent. And Hord stepped off the rock and out into the sea. Those men who had the watch on the king's ship saw the last of the king and Hord, and they never came up again.

And after this news the troops were signaled to disembark and hold a meeting. The news had now been heard by all the host that the king was dead, and so counsel was sought what to do with this great host. It seemed to the men that since King Ivar was dead, and they had no grievances against King Radbard, each would go home at once, since the wind was favorable. That advice to dissolve the war-levy was taken, and each man sailed to his own land.

And when Radbard heard this, he set Harald, his stepson, over some of his forces. Then Harald went with his host to Zealand, and he was accepted as king there. Next he went to Scania, to the kingdom that his mother's kinsmen had owned, and he was welcomed there and greatly strengthened his forces. Then he went up to Sweden and placed under himself all of the Swedish realm and Jutland, which Ivar, his mother's father, had ruled. Then he restored many petty kings who had formerly been deposed by King Ivar.

King Harald's rule was troublesome in the beginning, because he was a young man. Men thought it would be easy for them to try to retake their fathers' estates, which had been taken away by King Ivar or King Ingjald.

CHAPTER IV

Harald was fifteen years old when he was raised to the kingship. And because his friends knew that he would need much battle experience at a young age in order to defend the kingdom, it was decided to work a great magic spell, and King Harald was enchanted[12] so that iron would not bite him. And so it was that afterwards he never wore armor in battle, and yet no weapon touched him. He soon became a great warrior, and fought so many battles that no man of his kin had ever attained such warrior-ship in the kingdom but himself, and then he was called Harald Wartooth. He gained, by means of battles and raiding, all the realm that King Ivar had ruled, and so much more that there was not a king in Denmark or Sweden who didn't yield tribute to him; they all became his men. He conquered that portion of England that Halfdan the Valiant, and then King Ivar, had owned. He set up kings and jarls and made them yield tribute to him. He set King Hjormund, son of Hervard the Ylfing, over eastern Gautland, which his father and King Granmar had owned.[13]

CHAPTER V

At the time when King Harald Wartooth set himself up as the ruler of the kingdom of Sweden and Denmark, there was a king in Jutland who was named Hildibrand[14]. He was a powerful king and a great warrior. When he became old, he settled down on land. He had two children. His son was named Hildir, and his daughter was Hild. She was the loveliest of all maidens, and very proud in her mind.

When the king was very old, he became deathly ill. And when he was on the point of death, he called his son to him and counseled him with many pieces of good advice. He said that, first of all, he should marry off his sister somewhere far away; also, he should not share any portion of his land with her; and thirdly, he should not grant her any retainers, so that she might not maintain herself and her men by force. "Our meetings must now be ended. Keep the same friends as I have had, for you are a young man and lack foresight to govern the kingdom."

The king breathed his last, and the people summoned an assembly of many men, according to the law of the land. And at the assembly they set Hildir the king's son in the high seat and gave him the title of King. They swore fealty to him, and he swore to them to uphold the law of the land. After that, he prepared a great feast and inheritance-ale[15] in memory of his father, and a celebration for his friends. He gave titles to all his friends, and to the nobles who had previously served the old king.

When the kingdom was set in order in this way, Hild the king's daughter went before her brother, bowed to him and greeted him with blithe and fair words. She said. . .[16]

[The manuscript breaks off here and resumes with the visit of Hring, Harald's nephew]

CHAPTER VI

. . . he could raid. And one autumn he went to visit King Harald, his father's brother,[17] and he was warmly welcomed and stayed there for a while, highly honored. Because King Harald had grown very old, he put his kinsman Hring in command of the forces that defended his lands. Hring dwelled with Harald for a long time.

And when old age had begun to weigh down greatly on the king, then he set Hring, his kinsman, as king over Uppsala and gave him stewardship of all Sweden and west Gotland, but he himself held the rulership[18] of all Denmark and east Gotland. King Hring took to wife Alfhild, daughter[19] of King Alf, who ruled the land between two rivers, the Gautelf and the Raumelf. That was called Alfheim then.[20] It was a great forest. Hring had one son with his wife. He was called Ragnar.[21]

King Harald had two sons with his wife. One was Hraerek Ring-Slinger[22], and the other was Thrand the Old.[23]

CHAPTER VII

When King Harald Wartooth had become so old that he had lived a hundred and fifty years, he lay in bed and could not walk, and Vikings were coming to raid all over his kingdom. Then it seemed to his friends that the kingdom fared badly when the government began to fall apart, and he seemed to many to be old enough. Certain powerful men made a plan that when the king took a bath, they would lay wood on top of him and cover it with stones, and they would smother him in the bath.

When he found out that they wanted to put him to death, he then ordered that he be taken out of the bath. "I know that I seem to you all to be too old. And that is true, but I may as well die in the way that has been shaped for me. I don't want such a death—to die in the bath. I want to die in a much more kingly fashion." Then his friends came, and they took him away.

A little later, he sent men to Sweden to King Hring, his kinsman, with this message: that he should summon a host from all the kingdom that he defended, and come to meet him at the border and fight with him. He let it be known to him all the circumstances that had happened—how he seemed to the Danes to be too old.

After that, King Hring summoned a host from all the Swedish realm and west Gautland, and he had a great host from Norway. It is said that when the levy of Swedes and Norwegians sailed out from Stokksund[24], there were twenty-five hundred ships. Then King Hring rode with his guard and the West-Gauts over from the Øresund[25] and sought a path westward to the Kolmerk forest, which separate

Sweden from east Gautland. When King Hring came westwards out of the forests to the place called Bravik, his force of ships came to meet him there. And there King Hring set up his army tents, at Bravellir, beneath the forests and between the bays.

King Harald now collected together an army from the entire Danish realm, and a great host came out of Russia, and from Kvenland[26] and Germany. When his army was assembled together on Zealand at a place called Sygja, men could cross to Skåne from Landeyr just by walking on the ships. It seemed as if all the sea were thatched over with his host of ships. Then he sent the man named Herleif, and with him the contingent of Germans, to meet King Hring, and had them set up hazel stakes on the battlefield for him and claim the site for the battle,[27] and pronounce the breaking of peace and friendship. King Harold traveled with his army for seven days, until he had come east to Bravik. And then the two made ready for battle and deployed their forces.

CHAPTER VIII

It is said that in King Harald's army, there was a chieftain known as Bruni.[28] He was the wisest of all those men that were with him. Harald had Bruni deploy the troops and draw up the chieftains under the banner. King Harald's banner stood in the middle of the formation, and his personal guard surrounded his banner.

These champions were with King Harald: Svein, Sam, Gnepi the Old, Gard, Brand, Blæng, Teit, Tyrfing, Hjalti.[29] They were king Harald's skalds and champions. From King Harald's house guard there were Hjort, Borgar, Beli, Barri, Beigad, and Toki. There were the shield-maidens Visina and Heid,[30] and each had come with a great host to king Harald. Visina bore his standard. With her were the champions Kari and Milva. Vebjorg was the name of another shield-maiden who came to king Harald with a great host from the south, from Gotland, and many champions followed her. Of them all, the greatest and most famous were Ubbi the Frisian[31], Brat the Irish, Orm the English, Bui Bramuson, Ari the One-Eyed, and Geiralf. A great host of Wends[32] followed Visina the shield-maiden. They were easy to recognize: they had long swords and bucklers, but they did not have long shields like the other men.

On one of King Harald's flanks there was Heid the shield-maiden with her banner, and she had a hundred champions with her. There were her berserks: Grim, Geirr, Holmstein, Eysodul, Hedin the Slim, Dag the Livonian, and Harald Olafsson. There were many chieftains with Heid on that flank. On the other flank was that chieftain called Haki Cut-Cheek, and standards were borne before him. Many were the kings and champions with him. There were Alfar and Alfarin, the sons of King

Gandalf, who had already become King Harald's bodyguards and retainers. King Harald was in a wagon so that he might go to the battle, since he was not bearing weapons.

The king sent Bruni and Heid to spy out how Hring had arranged his forces and whether he was prepared for the battle. Bruni said, "It seems to me that Hring and his host are ready to fight. He has deployed his forces in an amazing way. He has arranged his battle lines in the boar's-head formation[33], and it won't be good to fight against him."

Then King Harald said, "Who could have taught Hring how to form the boar's-head formation? I thought that no one knew except for me and Odin[34]—or does Odin wish to deny me the gift of victory? That has never happened before, and still I pray to him that he not do that. But since he now does not wish to grant me victory, then may he let me fall in the battle with all my host, if he wills it not that the Danes have victory as before. And all the slain that fall on this field, I give to Odin."

It was as Bruni had said; Hring had formed all his host intothe boar's head formation. It seemed to the eye to be a very deep formation, since the point was in the forefront. However, it was so long that one flank began at the Var River, and the other one extended over to Bravik[35].

King Hring had with him in the battle many kings and champions. The greatest man with him was that king called Áli the Bold[36], who had a great multitude of men and many other famous kings and champions. With him was that champion who was the most famous in the old sagas, Starkad the Old, son of Storverk, who had been raised in Norway, in Hordaland on Fenring Island, and had traveled widely throughout the land and been with many kings. Many other champions had come from Norway to this battle: Thrand of Trondheim, Thorir of Mære, Helgi the White, Bjarni, Haf, Fid of the Fjord, Sigurd, Erling Snake from Jæderen, Saga-Eirik, Holmstein the White, Einar of Agder, Hrut the Waverer, Odd Wide-Traveler, Einar Snowshoe and Ivar Cape.

These were the great champions of King Hring: Aki, Eyvind, Egil the Squint-Eyed, Hildir, Gaut, Gudi Tolluson, Steinn of Vänern, and Styr the Strong. These also had their own company: Hrani Hildarson, Svein Shaved-Head, Hljombodi and Attack-Soti, Hrokkel Falcon, and Hrolf Woman-Chaser. There were also Dag the Fat, Gerdar the Glad, Duk the Wend, Glum of Värmland from west of the river, Saxi the Capable[37] and Sali of Gautland. These were from Sweden: Nori, Haki, Karl Beak, Krokar of the Meadow, Gunnfast, and Glismak the Good. These were from Sigtuna: Sigmund Market-Champion, Tolufrosti, Adils the Gaudy from Uppsala— he went out ahead of the banner and shields and was not in the ranks—and Sigvald, who had brought eleven ships to King Hring. Tryggvi and Tvivifil had come with twelve ships. Læsir had a warship, all occupied by champions. Eirik of Helsingland had a great dragon-ship, well crewed by warriors.

And there were men who'd come to King Hring from Telemark, who were champions, but who had the least respect because they seemed to be drawlers and slow speakers. These men were from there: Thorkel the Stubborn, Thorleif the Gotlander, Hadd the Hardy, Grettir the Twisted, and Hroald Toe. That man had also come to king Hring who was named Rognvald the Tall or Radbard Fist, the greatest of all champions. He was at the point of the wedge formation, and next to him were Tryggvi and Læsir, and on the outside were the Alrekssons and Yngvi. Then there were the men from Telemark, whom no one wanted to have; everyone thought they would be of little assistance. They were great bowmen.

CHAPTER IX

When this host was all deployed for battle, each side blew trumpets and screamed its loudest war-cry. Then the armies came together, and this battle was so fierce and so great, as is said in all the old sagas, that no battle has been fought in the Northlands with such a great number of such excellent men in the fight.

When the battle had just begun, the champion named Ubbi the Frisian advanced before King Harald's army, and he attacked the man who stood at the point of King Hring's formation. He had the first combat with Rognvald Redbeard, and their exchange was most fierce, and terrible blows might be seen there in the ranks when these bold men went at each other. Each gave the other many great blows, and Ubbi was such a great champion that he did not slacken until their single combat was ended, when Rognvald fell before him. And next he charged at Tryggvi and wounded him with a deadly wound. And when the Alrekssons saw how terrifying his onslaught was, they attacked him and fought with him, but he was so hardy and such a great champion that he killed both of them, and after that he killed Yngvi. And then he advanced into the ranks, so enraged that everyone whatsoever fled before him, and he felled all of those who stood foremost in the wedge, except for those who backed up against the other champions.

And when King Hring saw that, he urged his army not to let one man rout all such noble men as were with him—"but where is the champion Starkad, who has always borne the highest shield[38]? Win victory for us."

He answered, "We have more than enough work, lord, but we shall try to win such a victory as we may. But that man, Ubbi, may turn out to be a real trial."

But at the king's urging he charged out of the ranks against Ubbi, and there was a great battle between them, with huge blows and great strength, for both of them were bold. They fought for a while, and Starkad gave him one great wound, and in return he received six wounds, all large. It seemed to him that he had hardly ever had such a trial from one man. And because the ranks pressed so strongly, they were pushed in opposite directions, and thus their single combat was broken off.

Then Ubbi killed the champion named Agnar, and he constantly cleared a path before himself, striking with two hands. Both of his arms were bloody to the shoulders. And then he attacked the Telemark men. When they saw him, they said, "Now we don't need to look for any other position in the ranks. Let's attack this man with arrows for a while, and before. . . *[manuscript is missing 12-15 letters]* . . . the victory. And since it seems to everyone such a little thing that we came here, let's do all the more, so that we may seem bold men."

They began to shoot at him, they who were the bravest of the Telemark men, Hadd the Hardy and Hroald Toe. They were such bold men at shooting, that they shot two dozen arrows into his breast, and still he didn't die quickly. These men gave him his death—after he had killed six champions, and besides that had dealt great wounds to eleven champions, and had killed sixteen men of the Swedes and Gauts who stood in the front rank.

At that moment, Vebjorg the shieldmaiden made a great attack against the Swedes and Gauts. She charged at the champion called Attack-Soti, and she had trained herself so much with helm and byrnie and sword that she was the foremost in knighthood, as Starkad the Old says. She struck champions with mighty blows, and attacked for a long time. She struck one blow on his cheek and chopped his jawbone apart and sliced off his chin. He tucked his beard in his mouth and bit down on it and so held his chin up. She accomplished many great deeds in the ranks. A little while later Thorkel the Stubborn, a champion of King Hring, met her, and they exchanged fierce attacks, and before it was over he killed her with great wounds, and much courage.[39]

Now many great events happened in a short time. Each army by turns held the advantage. Many a man on both sides never came home, or received lasting scars.

Now Starkad rushed forward at the Danes. He attacked the champion named Hun and they battled each other. In the end Starkad killed him and, a little later, the one who tried to avenge him, named Ella. And then he advanced on the one named Borgar; they had a hard combat together, and in the end Starkad killed him. Starkad now charged the ranks with drawn sword and struck down one man after another. And next he struck down the one named Hjort, and then Visina the shield-maiden met him; she bore King Harald's banner. Starkad attacked her fiercely.

Then she said to Starkad, "Now Hel's greed has come upon you, and now you must die, you ogre."[40]

He answered, "But first, you'll let King Harald's banner droop," and he cut off her left hand. Then the man called Brai, the father of Sækalf, came against him to avenge her, and Starkad ran him through with his sword. Now one might see great heaps of corpses in the ranks, far and wide.

Somewhat later, Gnepja, a great champion, came against Starkad, and they attacked each other fiercely, and Starkad gave him a death-wound. Next he killed the champion named Haki, and he got the greatest wound in that moment. He was slashed between his neck and shoulders, so that his insides could be seen, and on the front of his chest he had such a great wound that his lungs were falling out, and he had lost a finger on the right hand.[41]

When King Harald saw how great was the slaughter of his men and champions, he raised himself up on his knees and picked up two knives and harshly whipped forward the horse that was hitched to the wagon. He thrust with both blades with both hands and dealt death to many men with his own hands, even though he could not walk nor sit on a horse.[42] The battle now went on for a while, as the king accomplished many mighty deeds.

Towards the end of this battle, King Harald Wartooth was slain by a club to the head, shattering his skull. That was his death-blow, and Bruni killed him.[43] King Hring saw King Harald's wagon empty, and he realized that the king must have fallen. He ordered trumpets to be blown and called for the hosts to stand down. When the Danes became aware of this, they stopped fighting, and King Hring offered a truce to all of King Harald's army, and they all accepted it.

The next day, in the morning, King Hring ordered a search among the slain for the body of King Harald, his kinsman. There was a great host of dead fallen over where the body lay. It happened that the broken body was found at mid-day. King Hring had the body of King Harald, his kinsman, taken and cleaned of blood and prepared with full honors, according to the ancient custom. He had the body lie in the wagon which King Harald had in the battle. And after that he had a great howe raised up[44], and then had King Harald ride in the wagon, hitched to the horse which he had in the battle. And so he had him ride into the howe, and then the horse was killed. Then King Hring took the saddle which he himself had ridden on, and he gave it to King Harald, his kinsman, and bade him do whichever he wished: ride on horseback to Valhall, or ride in the wagon. Then he had a great feast made there, and conducted the funeral rites for King Harald, his kinsman.

And before the howe was shut, King Hring bid all the great men and all the champions that were present to come and cast great rings and good weapons into the howe, for the honor of King Harald Wartooth. And after that the howe was carefully closed.

CHAPTER X

Sigurd Hring was king over Sweden and Denmark after King Harald Wartooth. His son, Ragnar, grew up among his father's guard. He was the tallest and most handsome of all men that anyone had seen. He was like his mother and her kin in appearance, for it is known, in all the old tales about that folk called the alfar, that they were much more handsome than any other people in the Northlands. For all the ancestors of Alfhild, his mother, and all her lineage, had descended from Alf the Old. That was called the alf-clan then. From him is taken the name of the two great rivers which have both been called *elfs* since then. One separated his kingdom from Gotland and for this reason was called the Gautelf, and the other flowed through the land that is now called Romerike, and was called Raumelf.[45] Ragnar resembled his own father and his father's kin in being tall, as King Harald Wartooth and Ivar Wide-Grasp had been.

When King Hring began to grow old and decrepit, his kingdom began to diminish, and the part that had first belonged to him diminished the most. There was a king named Æthelberht, who was descended from the kin of King Ælle, the one who killed Halfdan the Ylfing. He laid under his rule that portion of England which was called Northumbria. King Hring and also King Harald had held that portion. King Æthelberht ruled that kingdom for a long time. His sons were named Ama and Ælle, who were kings in Northumbria after their father.

When Sigurd Hring was old, one autumn he had ridden through his own kingdom, western Gautland, to render judgment on men according to the law of the land. Then the sons of Gandalf, his in-laws, came to meet him and asked him to help them to ride against that king who was called Eystein, who ruled over the kingdom which then was called Vestmar and is now called Vestfold. Then a sacrifice was held in Skiringssal[46], to which people came from all over Viken[47]. . .

LIST OF SWEDISH KINGS

[Sigvard Ring] took as his wife Alfhild, the great-granddaughter of Alf, a king in Norway, known as "the Old". Alf the Old (Alfuren gamle) was born of his father Raum, and was the grandson of Nor, the first king of Norway (see the genealogy of the Norwegian kings).[1] When the kingdom, after the passing of Nor, was divided into small provinces again, that king was allotted a portion which lies between two of the more prominent rivers in Norway, and which in that language is called Alfheim. From Alf these rivers were given the name Elffve in the common language. Later their names were specifically distinguished: the Raumelffve and the Gautelffve.

The kin of Alfhild was called the alf-kin or alf-clan. That folk in ancient days was much more beautiful than any other people, and so were their descendants.[2]

By Alfhild, Sigvard Ring had a son, Ragner Lodbrog, of whom more later. When Alfhild was dead, Sigurd decided to marry another woman. For when he had crossed the sea from Vestrogotia, a province of his kingdom, to the province of Vichia in Norway for the performance of folk rites which were to be celebrated in Sciringsal, he saw the most beautiful virgin Alfsol, the daughter of King Alf of Vendel. He immediately fell in love with her and longed for the girl whom he had seen, and he wholly wanted to gain the one he desired, even though it was completely against the will of the Gods.

One of her brothers was named Alf, after his father, and the other was Ingvi. Sigvard asked them for permission to marry their sister. They refused to hand over the most beautiful young girl to a wrinkled old man. The King was enraged that such a monarch as himself was going to be rejected by the sons of a petty king, and he threatened bloody war. In fact, it is not permitted to fight a duel in the presence of the sacred rites. Therefore he called for war, a little while after the brothers had spoken. Although the brothers were most famous for their wisdom and their deeds, upon learning of the very numerous army of Sigvard before they set out for the battle, they gave their sister poison to drink, so that she would not become spoils of victory.

Then after a fierce fight in which Alf and his brother Ingvone were killed, Sigvard himself was badly wounded. When Alfsol's funeral procession was brought, he boarded a great ship loaded with dead bodies, as the only living person. Placing himself and the dead Alfsol in the stern, he ordered the ship to be burned with pitch, tar and sulfur. With sails raised high, pushed away from the land by strong winds, he steered the prow, and at the same time his hand did violence to himself. With an excited spirit, he had previously said to his companions left behind on the shore that he, the achiever of so many deeds, possessor of such kingdoms, chose to visit King Odinus (that is, the underworld) with a royal procession, according to the custom of his own forefathers, rather than endure the infirmity of an inactive old age. (Some tell about him that before he left the shore, he stabbed himself with his own hand). Nonetheless, he had a mound heaped up on the shore of the sea, according to the custom of the time, which he ordered to be called Ringshaug.[3] With his vessel truly steered by storms, he himself crossed the waves of the Styx without delay.

[Ragner] was the third possessor of the royal power in continuous line of descent from Ivar Viidfadma.[4] His provinces were invaded everywhere by neighboring princes who heard that his father was dead and were less afraid of Ragner in adolescence. Men advised him to expand his marital alliance and to ask for Thora, the daughter of Gautric, the baron of Gautland. And so, having bravely killed a snake of uncommonly large size, he kept the reward with which the baron repaid him. She died thereafter, leaving behind two sons, Eric and Agner. Lodbrok recovered all the ancestral provinces of his kingdom.

After many years of war in neighboring parts of Europe, so that he might increase the brightness of his name by his deeds, he entered into a second marriage, his first wife being dead. He took to wife one Aslauga, whose father was the most famous fighter in Europe, Sigvard, descended from the King of Sweden. His nickname was Foffnisbane, which is to say, "serpent-killer". Foffnir, or Fophnyr (not unlike the Greek *ophis*) meant "serpent" or "snake" in Norwegian. From this marriage Ragner had five sons: Ivar was born the oldest; Witserc; Biorn; Raugnvald (who fell in adolescence, in the army of his brothers), and Sigvard, born the youngest of those remaining. At a suitable age they invaded kingdoms of moderate size, as will be spoken of briefly later. Every year Ragner was away, enlarging the boundaries of his kingdom by arms, and he left Sweden in the care of a certain Eysten. Ragner's sons from his first marriage, Eric and Agner, had tried to invade their father's kingdom unjustly.

THE TALE OF RAGNAR'S SONS

CHAPTER I

After the death of King Hring, his son Ragnar assumed the kingship over the realms of the Swedes and the Danes. Then many kings came to the kingdom and subjected it to their rule, because he was a young man, and he seemed to them to be hardly fit for wise counsel or governing.

There was one jarl in West Gautland who was named Herraud. He was a jarl of King Ragnar. He was the wisest of men, and a great warrior. He had one daughter who was called Thora Fortress-Hart. She was the loveliest woman that the king had ever heard of. The jarl, her father, had given her a little snake as a morning-gift[1]. At first she raised it in her little box, but after a while this snake became so large that it lay in a ring around her bower and bit its own tail. It became so savage that people didn't dare to come near the bower, except for those who gave it food or served the jarl's daughter—and it ate an ox each day. The people were greatly terrified, and they knew that it would do great harm, as huge and as savage as it had become. The Jarl then swore this most solemn oath[2]: that he should give his daughter, Thora, to the one man who would kill the snake, or who would dare to go and talk with her in front of the snake.

When King Ragnar heard this news, he went to West Gautland. And when he had only a short way to go to the jarl's estate, he set out in shaggy clothes, breeches and a cape with sleeves and a hood. These clothes were matted with sand and tar. He took a great spear in his hand and was girded with a sword, and so he left his own men and went alone to the jarl's estate and Thora's bower. And as soon as the snake saw that an unknown man had come, it reared up and blew venom against him. But he blocked it with his shield, and boldly went at the snake and killed it with his spear in its heart. Then he drew his sword and hewed off the snake's head. And it turned out, as is said in the *Saga of King Ragnar*, that he married Thora Fortress-Hart, and then he set out on a campaign and freed all his kingdom.

He had two sons with Thora; one was named Eirik, and the other Agnar. When they were a few years old, Thora fell sick and breathed her last. After that Ragnar took to wife Aslaug, whom some called Randalin, the daughter of Sigurd Fafnir's-Bane and Brynhild Budli's-Daughter. They had four sons. Ivar the Boneless was the oldest, then Bjorn Ironsides, then Hvitserk, then Sigurd. There was a mark in his eye like a serpent lying around the pupil, and for that he was called Sigurd Snake-in-the-Eye.

CHAPTER II

Now when the sons of Ragnar were grown, they raided widely in many lands. Their brothers Eirik and Agnar traveled to separate places, and Ivar went to a third stead and his younger brothers with him, and he made plans for them, because he was very clever. They took for themselves Zealand and Jutland, Gotland and Öland and all the islands in the sea. Ivar and his younger brothers set themselves up at Lejre on Zealand, although that was against King Ragnar's will. His sons went raiding everywhere, because they didn't want to be less famous than King Ragnar, their father.

King Ragnar didn't like it that his sons resisted him and took his tribute-paying lands against his will. He set a king called Eystein Beli over Upper Sweden, and told him to take care of his kingdom, but to defend against his sons if they laid claim to it.

One summer, when King Ragnar had gone with his host to the Baltic[3], his sons Eirik and Agnar came to Sweden and moored their ships in Lake Mälaren.[4] They sent a message to Uppsala for King Eystein to come to them. And when they met, Eirik said that he wanted King Eystein to rule Sweden under the brothers' lordship, and asked to marry Borghild, his daughter, and said that then they could hold the kingdom well, instead of King Ragnar.[5] Eystein said that he wanted to present this to the local chieftains, and so they parted.

When King Eystein brought up this case, all the landed-men reached an agreement to defend the land against Ragnar's sons. An overwhelming force was summoned, and King Eystein went out against Ragnar's sons. When they encountered each other, there was a great battle, and the sons of Lodbrok were overpowered, and so many fell on the brothers' side that only a few were left standing. Agnar fell, and Eirik was taken prisoner.

King Eystein promised Eirik safe conduct, and as much wealth as he might wish from the Uppsala treasury as compensation for his brother Agnar, and along with that, his daughter, whom he had previously asked for. Eirik wanted no compensation and no king's daughter, and said that he didn't wish to live after the defeat he had suffered—but he said that he would accept the right to choose his own death-day for himself. Because King Eystein could not reach a settlement with Eirik, he agreed to that. Eirik asked that they put the points of their spears under him and lift him up over all the fallen. Then Eirik said:

I'll won't take brother's blood-money,
nor buy a maiden with rings.
It's now said that Eystein
has become Agnar's bane.
My mother won't mourn me;
I'll mount up high above the slain.
Let the greedy spear-shaft
skewer me right through.

Before he was heaved up on the spears, he saw a man riding fast. Then he said:

Fare with my final words—
finished are eastern journeys—
the slender lady Aslaug
now owns my hoard of rings.
Fury will be fiercest
when they find out my death,
if my stepmother speaks of it
to her sons so gentle.

Now it was done: Eirik was lifted up on the spear-points, and thus he died, up above the slain.

When Aslaug heard the news on Zealand, at once she went to meet her sons and tell them the news. Bjorn and Hvitserk were playing a boardgame there, and Sigurd stood before them. Then Aslaug said:

Had you been first to fall,
without fail you would not
be lying, lacking vengeance,
half a year later, brothers,
if Eirik and Agnar
—I'll conceal it little—
brethren not born of me,
still did breathe and live.

Then Sigurd Snake-in-the-Eye answered:

It will take us three weeks,
if you are troubled, mother—

far must be our faring—
for our forces to be ready.
If sword-edges aid us,
Eystein Beli shall not
hold Uppsala's high seat,
though hoarded wealth he offer.

Then Bjorn Ironsides said:

A hawk-keen breast, holding
bold heart and mind within,
aids a man, though he make
but little mention of it.
Though no snakes nor serpents
shimmer in our own eyes,
my brothers made me merry,
I remember your stepsons.

Then Hvitserk answered:

Let's plan before we promise,
plot to wreak our vengeance,
be blithe that Agnar's banesman
must bear a host of harms;
let's launch the boat on the billows,
break ice before the prow,
see how soon we can get
our sailing ships outfitted.

Then Ivar the Boneless said:

You all boast of boundless
bravery and daring.
Now what you all need is
great tenacity as well.
I'll be hoisted above heroes,
because I have no bones, yet
I'll have a hand in vengeance,
whichever I make use of.

After that, Ragnar's sons assembled an overwhelming force. When they were ready, they traveled with a fleet of ships to Sweden, but Queen Aslaug travelled overland with fifteen hundred knights, and that force was very well equipped. She herself wore armor and commanded this army, and was called Randalin. They met up in Sweden, and plundered and burned everywhere they went.

King Eystein heard about that, and summoned every man in his kingdom who could fight to join forces against them. And when they met, there was a great battle; Lodbrok's sons won the victory, but King Eystein fell. That story was told and retold, and has become very famous.

King Ragnar heard the news as he was raiding, and he was very displeased with his sons because they had not let their revenge wait for him. And when he came home to his kingdom, he said to Aslaug that he would do no fewer famous deeds than his sons had done. "I have now won back under my rule almost all the kingdom that my ancestors had, except for England, and for that, I have now had two transports built in Lidar, in Vestfold"[6]—because all his kingdom lay between the Dovrefjell[7] and Lindesnes.[8]

Aslaug answered, "You might have had many longships made there for the cost of these transports. Know this as well: it's no good to sail for England in large vessels, on account of the currents and sandbars. This is not being planned wisely."

But all the same, King Ragnar traveled west to England in these ships with five hundred men, and he wrecked both ships on the coast of England, but he himself and all his forces came safely to land. He now took to harrying wherever he went.

CHAPTER III

At that time, a king named Ælle ruled over Northumbria. When he heard that a host had come to his kingdom, he summoned a huge army, and went out and attacked them with overwhelming force, and there was a great and hard battle there. On the outside of his clothes, King Ragnar wore the silk tunic which Aslaug gave him at their parting. Because the defending forces were so large that no one might withstand them, nearly all his folk fell there, but he himself went four times right through King Ælle's ranks, and no iron pierced his silk shirt. He was finally captured and placed in an enclosure full of snakes, and the snakes didn't want to come near him. King Ælle saw that no iron had bitten him by day, when they fought each other, and now none of the snakes wanted to injure him. He ordered the clothing which Ragnar had worn outermost that day to be stripped off him. The snakes immediately latched onto him everywhere, and he laid down his life with great valor.

When the sons of King Ragnar heard the news, they went west to England and fought with King Ælle. And because neither Ivar nor any of his folk would fight, and the defenders were more numerous, they suffered a defeat there and fled to their ships. With matters as they stood, they went home to Denmark.

But afterwards, Ivar was in England and went to meet King Ælle, and asked him for compensation for his father. And since King Ælle saw that Ivar would not fight together with his brothers against him, it seemed safe to reach a settlement with him.[9] Ivar asked the king to give him, as compensation for his father, as much land as he might span with the largest old bull's hide, because he said that it would not be good for him to go home to face his brothers without a settlement. This didn't seem treacherous to Ælle, and they bound themselves to this agreement.

Ivar now took a raw hide and had it stretched as much as possible. He had the hide cut into the finest cord, and then he split the hair side from the flesh side. Then he had the cord drawn around a flat field and marked a foundation all around the outside. He raised up strong city walls there, and this city is now called York[10]. He made friends with all the folk of the land and especially with the chieftains, and so it came to be that all the chieftains called him and his brothers trustworthy. Then he sent an invitation to his brothers and said that right then they would have the best chance to avenge their father, if they came with a host to England. When they heard that, they called up their forces and sailed for England.

When Ivar became aware of this, he went at once to meet King Ælle, and said that he would not hide such news from him, but he could not fight against his own brothers; however, he would go to meet with them and try to reach a settlement. The king accepted that. Ivar came to meet his brothers and encouraged them to avenge their father, and a little later went to King Ælle and said that they were so savage and furious that they wanted to fight more than anything else. What Ivar had done appeared to the king to be the greatest faithfulness. The king moved against the brothers with his army. And when they came together, many chieftains turned from the king to Ivar. The king was overcome by overwhelming force: the better part of his army fell, and he himself was captured.[11]

Ivar and the brothers now remembered how their father had been tortured. They had an eagle carved on Ælle's back, and then had all the ribs severed from the backbone with a sword, so that the lungs were pulled out. So said the skald Sighvat in his *Praise-Poem for King Knut*:[12]

And Ivar
who resided at York
ordered Ælle's back
carved by an eagle.[13]

After this battle Ivar made himself king over that portion of England that his kinfolk had held before. He had two brothers who were sons of a concubine, one named Yngvar and the other Husto.[14] They tortured the holy King Edmund[15] on Ivar's orders, and then Ivar took over his kingdom.[16]

The sons of Lodbrok went raiding in many lands: England and Wales and France[17] and as far as Lombardy. It is said that the most distant place they went was when they conquered the city called Luna. And at one time they intended to go to Rome and conquer it. Their raid has become the most famous tale in the Norse tongue, in all the Northlands.

When they came back to Denmark, their own kingdom, they divided up their lands among themselves. Bjorn Ironsides took the kingdom of Uppsala and all Sweden and their dependencies.[18] Sigurd Snake-in-the-Eye had Zealand and Skåne and Halland and all Viken[19] and Agder as far as Lindesnes and the greater part of Uppland. Hvitserk had Jutland and Wendland[20].

Sigurd Snake-in-the-Eye married Blaeja, the daughter of King Ælle.[21] Their son was Knut, who was called Horda-Knut[22], and who took over the rule of Zealand, Skåne and Halland after his father—but Viken broke away from him then. He had one son who was named Gorm. He was named after his foster-father, the son of Knut the Foundling, who ruled all the lands of the sons of Ragnar while they were away raiding. Gorm Knutsson was the largest and strongest of all men, and the most accomplished man in all affairs, but he was not as wise as his forebears had been.[23]

CHAPTER IV

Gorm took the kingship after his father. He married Thyra, who was called Denmark's Benefit[24], the daughter of Klakk-Harald[25] who was king in Jutland. And when Harald died, Gorm laid all that kingdom under his own rule. King Gorm went with an army over all of Jutland and killed all the sea-kings, all the way south to the Schlei River, and thus he conquered much of Wendland. He fought many battles with the Saxons, and he became the mightiest of kings.[26] He had two sons. The elder was named Knut, and the younger was Harald. Knut was the most handsome man that people had ever seen. The king loved him more than anyone, and so did all the people. He was called the Danes' Beloved. Harald resembled his mother's kin, and his mother loved him no less than Knut.

Ivar the Boneless was king for a long time in England. He had no children, because he was so constituted that he had no lust nor love in him, but he didn't lack cunning or cruelty. He died of old age in England and was buried there in a howe.

70

Then all of the sons of Lodbrok were dead.

After Ivar, Æthelmund took the kingdom in England. He was the nephew of Saint Edmund, and he spread Christianity widely in England. He imposed a tax on Northumbria because it was heathen. After him, his son, who was named Æthelberht[27], took the kingdom. He was a good king and lived to be old. Near the end of his days, the Danish army came to England, and the leaders of the army were Knut and Harald, the sons of King Gorm.[28] They placed under their rule a large kingdom in Northumbria, which Ivar had held. King Æthelberht went against them, and they fought north of Cleveland, and many of the Danes fell there.

Some time later, the Danes came up against Scarborough, and they fought there and won a victory. Then they went south to York, and all the folk submitted to them, and they feared nothing. One day, when the weather was hot, men went swimming. And as the king's sons were swimming among the ships, men rushed down from the land and shot at them. Knut was struck by an arrow and killed, and his men took the body and carried it out to the ships.[29] When the men on land saw that, they banded together, so that the Danes would have no place to land because of the assembled men, and then would go back home to Denmark.

King Gorm was in Jutland then. When he heard these tidings, he collapsed, and he died of grief at the same time the next day. Harald, his son, took the rulership of the Danish realm after him. He was the first of his kin to accept the faith and be baptized.[30]

CHAPTER V

Sigurd Snake-in-the-Eye and Bjorn Ironsides and Hvitserk had harried widely in France. Then Bjorn turned home to his kingdom. After that, the emperor Arnulf[31] fought with the brothers, and a hundred thousand Danes and Norwegians fell there. Sigurd Snake-in-the-Eye fell there, and another king fell there whose name was Gudrod. He was the son of Olaf, the son of Hring, the son of Ingjald, the son of Ingi, the son of Hring, whom Ringerike is named after. Hring was the son of Dag and Thora Mother-of-Warriors.[32] They had nine sons, and from them are descended the clan of the Döglings.

Gudrod's brother was named Helgi the Keen. He had brought the banner of Sigurd Snake-in-the-Eye, and his sword and shield, out of the battle. He traveled home to Denmark with his forces and there met Aslaug, Sigurd's mother, and told her the news. Then Aslaug spoke a verse:

> The seekers after the slain°
> sit on the fortress-neck°;

seekers after the slain: ravens
fortress-neck: walls

a shame that the swart raven
leaves Sigurd's namesake unavenged.[33]
Let the body's blithe enjoyers° [34]   *body's enjoyers:* flames
blaze on the wood-chips around him;
all too soon, Odin let
the alf of the Valkyries° die.   *alf of the Valkyries:* warrior

But because Horda-Knut was young, Helgi stayed there with Aslaug a long time to defend the country.

Sigurd and Blaeja had a daughter. She was Horda-Knut's twin. Aslaug gave her her own name and raised her up and later fostered her. She was later married to Helgi the Keen. Their son was Sigurd Hart[35]. He was the most handsome and greatest and strongest of anyone that men had ever seen. Gorm Knutsson and Sigurd Hart were of the same age. When Sigurd was twelve years old, he killed a berserk named Hildibrand in single combat, and then his band—twelve people, all together. After that, Klakk-Harald gave him his own daughter, named Ingibjorg. They had two children, Gudthorm and Ragnhild.

Then Sigurd found out that King Frodi, his father's brother, was dead. He went north to Norway and made himself king over Ringerike, his own inheritance. There is a long saga about him, for he accomplished many sorts of brave deeds. But there is this to tell about his death: he rode out into the wilderness to hunt animals, as was his custom, and there Haki the Hadeland-Berserk came against him with thirty fully armed men and fought with him. Sigurd fell there. He had already killed twelve men, while King Haki lost his right hand and received three more wounds.

After that, King Haki rode with his men to Ringerike, to Stein, which was Sigurd's home, and he took away Ragnhild his daughter and his son Gudthorm, and much property besides, and carried them home with him to Hadeland. A little later, he had arrangements made for a great feast, and intended to hold his wedding, but that was delayed because his wounds were doing poorly. Ragnhild was then fifteen years old, and Gudthorm was fourteen. So autumn and winter passed until Yule, as Haki lay wounded.

King Halfdan the Black was at Heidmark at his estates. He sent Harek Wand, and a hundred men with him. They traveled over the ice on Lake Mjøsa to Hadeland in one night, and came during the day to King Haki's farmstead, and blocked all the doors of the house where his guard was sleeping. Then they went to King Haki's sleeping quarters and took Ragnhild and Gudthorm her brother and all the possessions that were there, and carried them off. They burned the hall and all the guardsmen in it, and then went away. King Haki stood up and dressed, and pursued them for a while. When he came to the ice on the lake, he turned the hilt of his sword downwards and fell on the point, and got his death. He is laid in a mound there, at the water's edge.

King Halfdan saw them driving over the ice in a covered wagon, and he realized that their mission must have turned out just as he wished. He had a message sent to all the settlements and invited the great men in Heidmark to the celebrations, and held a great feast that day. He then made a wedding feast for Ragnhild, and after that they were together for many a day. Their son was King Harald Fairhair, who became the first sole king over all Norway.

KRÁKUMÁL

1. We struck with our swords!
So long ago, it was:
we had gone to Gautland
for the ground-wolf's° slaughter.　　　　　　　　　　*ground-wolf:* serpent
Then we won fair Thora;
thus the warriors named me
Lodbrok, when I laid that
heather-eel° low in battle,　　　　　　　　　　　　*heather-eel:* serpent
ended the earth-coil's° life　　　　　　　　　　　　*earth-coil:* serpent
with inlaid shining steel.

2. We struck with our swords!
Still was I young, when we
went east to Øresund,[1]
carved the eager wolf's meal.
We gave a great dinner
to the gold-legged birds,°　　　　　　　　　　　　*gold-legged birds:* eagles
where hard iron clashed, howling
against helmets, tall and well forged.
All the sea was swollen,
in slain-blood the raven waded.

3. We struck with our swords!
Spears we held high, when we
were rightly reckoned twenty,
reddened blades far and wide.
Eight earls we defeated
eastwards on the Danube,
fed the wolf, from that fight,
a fine meal in plenty.
Wound-sweat° swelled the ocean,　　　　　　　　　　*wound-sweat:* blood
swordsmen laid their lives down.

4. We struck with our swords!
Surely Hedin's wife° came,[2]   *Hedin's wife*: battle
when we hastened the Helsings
to the hall of Odin;
we anchored on the Iva,[3]
awful spearheads bit then,
that river was all reddened
with hot running wound-splash°.   *wound-splash*: blood
Blade howled against byrnie,
bane-herrings° clett shields[4].   *bane-herrings*: swords

5. We struck with our swords!
I suppose no one withstood us,
until, on Heflir's horses°,   *Heflir*: a sea-king; his *horses*: ships
Herrod fell in the fight.
No prouder earl ever ploughed
the puffins' field°, none ever   *puffins' field*: the sea
sailed on Ægir's snowshoes°   *Ægir*: sea god; his *snowshoes*: ships
to ships' harbor, since then.
That king bore a brave heart
in battles far and wide.

6. We struck with our swords!
Soldiers flung their shields down
where corpse-cur° carved its way,   *corpse-cur*: sword
cleaving breasts of warriors;
strife-blades bit in struggle
at the Skarpa Skerries[5];
round-shields' moon° was reddened   *shields' moon*: sword
before King Rafn fell.
Wound-sweat° welled from men's skulls,   *wound-sweat*: blood
spattered warriors' mailcoats.

7. We struck with our swords!
Swinging blades were howling
before King Eystein fell there
on the Field of Ullr[6];
we went, glittering with gold
of the ground of the falcon°—   *ground of the falcon*: arm

corpse-light° shattered shield-boards—   *corpse-light*: sword
from ships to helm-meeting°;   *helm-meeting*: battle
neck-ale° burst from blade wounds,   *neck-ale*: blood
from brain-cliffs° it spurted.   *brain-cliffs*: heads

8. We struck with our swords!
We stood on Inndyr's island;
ravens reaped a bounty
of raw meat to butcher.
We fed to Fala's horses°   *Fala*: a giantess; her *horses*: wolves
full meals, for the time being
—hard to shield one soldier—
at the sun's arising;
I saw bowstring-stakes° soar,   *bowstring-stakes*: arrows
metal splitting helm-seams.

9. We struck with our swords!
We smeared our shields with gore
before Bornholm, where we
banqueted wound-starlings°;   *wound-starlings*: ravens
blade's battle-cloud° shattered,   *blade's battle-cloud*: shield
bows flung metal far off.
Volnir fell in the fighting,
no finer king ever was.
The wolf welcomed our offering
of corpse-windrows along the shore.

10. We struck with our swords!
Strife had clearly grown great
when King Frey had fallen
in the Flemings' country;
the bitter, black wound-hoe°,   *wound-hoe*: sword
with blood all enamelled,
cut gilt cowls of Hogni°   *Hogni*: a famous king; his *cowl*: chainmail
in combat, long ago;
women wailed that morning
as wolves received our sacrifice.

11. We struck with our swords!
The slain lay by the hundreds

at Englanes, as it's called,
on Eynaefi's snowshoes.°   *Eynaefi*: a sea-king: his *snowshoes*: ships
We sailed to the slaughter
six days before the host fell,
celebrated at sunrise
the solemn Mass of arrows°;[7]   *Mass* [i.e. Christian worship service] *of arrows*: battle
Valthjof bent in battle,
bowed before our weapons.

12. We struck with our swords!
There streamed from our blades
brown dew of pale bodies°   *dew of bodies*: blood
in Bardafjord, for hawks;
bows whined, as the bolt points
bit most deeply into
Svolnir's hammer-forged shirts°   *Svolnir*: Odin; his *shirts*: chainmail
in scabbard-flames'° quarrel;   *scabbard-flames*: drawn swords
smeared with sweat°, envenomed,   *sweat*: blood
the wound-serpent° struck home.   *wound-serpent*: sword

13. We struck with our swords!
Hlokk's shelters° we brandished,   *Hlokk*: a valkyrie; her *shelters*: shields
held them high in Hild's game°,   *Hild*: a valkyrie; her *game*: battle
there at Hjadninga Bay;[8]
surely men could see then
the shattered helms of warriors,
as we broke through bucklers
in the brawl of corpse-fish°—   *corpse-fish*: swords
not like lying with a lovely
lady in bed beside you.[9]

14. We struck with our swords!
Storms° pounded on armor,   *storms*: battle
corpses fell on the field
in fair Northumbria;
no one needed to refuse,
as the night was ending,
Hild's game, where helm-stumps°   *helm-stumps*: heads
were hewn by keen light-flickers°—   *light-flickers*: drawn swords
not like kissing, comforting
a comely widow in the high seat.

15. We struck with our swords!
So it then was destined:
Herthjof held the victory
in the Hebrides, against us;
Rognvald met his ruin
before the rain of shields°,   *rain of shields:* battle
the greatest came to grief there
in the gusts of swords°;   *gusts of swords:* battle
helm-shaker° shot swiftly   *helm-shaker:* warrior
the string-notched palm trees°.   *string-notched palm trees:* arrows

16. We struck with our swords!
The slain lay athwart each other;
the spear-clash's cuckoo°   *spear-clash's cuckoo:* raven
was cheered by the sword-play;
when metal blades met shields,
King Marstan, lord of Ireland,
never suffered the she-wolf
to starve, nor the eagle;
the greedy raven was given
gore-sacrifice at Waterford.

17. We struck with our swords!
I saw a host that morning
bow before the blade's edge
in the brawl of spearpoints°;   *rawl of spearpoints:* battle
too soon, my son was hurt by
scabbard-thorn° in his heart;   *scabbard-thorn:* sword
from unafraid Agnar
Egil stole the life-breath;
spear smashed against Hamdir's
gray sark°; banners shimmered.   *Hamdir:* a warrior; his *sark:* chainmail

18. We struck with our swords!
I saw Endil's trusty offspring°   *Endil:* a sea-king; his *offspring:* warriors
slice up no scant morsels
with their swords, for the wolf.
It was not like women
bringing wine, at Vikaskeid[10]:
Ægir's donkey° dripped blood   *Ægir:* sea god; his *donkey:* ship

in the din of spears°, no little;   *din of spears*: battle
Skogul's cape° was scoured   *Skogul*: a valkyrie; her *cape*: chainmail
in the Skjoldungs'° fury.   *Skjoldungs*: kings (Danish dynasty)

19. We struck with our swords!
We sported with our weapons,
a morning match with three
mighty lords, at Lindisey;
few enjoyed good fortune—
many fell into wolf's jaws
that fought for flesh with the hawk—
to fare whole from there;
Irish blood was blended
with brine, at the slaughter.

20. We struck with our swords!
I saw the maiden's swain,
fair-haired lover of lasses,
lying dead that morning.
It wasn't like a warm bath
that the wine-beaker-Njorun°   *Njorun*: goddess; *beaker-Njorun*: woman
might draw for us, down in Álasund[11]
before the death of King Oru;
I saw the battle-moon° burst,   *battle-moon*: shield
broken were lives of men.

21. We struck with our swords!
Swinging blades bit bucklers,
where the gilt spear glanced off
against the bark of Hild°.   *Hild*: a valkyrie; her *bark*: armor
Ever since, on Anglesey
it may be seen clearly
how the captains came forth
to the contest of blades°;   *contest of blades*: battle
flying wyrm-of-wounds° was   *wyrm of wounds*: spear
wet with blood, on the bank.

22. We struck with our swords!
Why should a warrior cower
before the ranks, when braving

the blizzard of spearpoints°?
He who mourns his demise has
never fed meat often
to eagles in the edge-game.°
It's hard to urge on weaklings;
no coward takes courage
from his craven heart.

blizzard of spearpoints: battle

edge-game: battle

23. We struck with our swords!
I say it's right for a lad
to dare to dash at foemen
as they draw swords together.
Let thane not shrink from thane—
that long was the warriors' way;
maids' darlings should be dauntless
in the din of swords°, always.

din of swords: battle

24. We struck with our swords!
It seems to me an ordeal
that our fates we must follow;
few escape the Norns' craft.
I didn't imagine Ælle
as the end of my life,
when I fed blood-falcons°
and forced keels through the water—
we gave wolves worthy payment
widely, in Scotland's bays.

blood-falcons: ravens

25. We struck with our swords!
My soul is glad, for I know
that Balder's father's° benches
for a banquet are made ready.
We'll toss back toasts of ale
from bent trees of the skulls°;[12]
no warrior bewails his death
in the wondrous house of Fjolnir°.
Not one word of weakness
will I speak in Vidrir's° hall.

Balder's father: Odin

trees of the skulls: drinking horns

Fjolnir: Odin

Vidrir: Odin

26. We struck with our swords!
The sons of Aslaug all would

rouse the wrath of Hild° here
with their ruthless sword-blades,
if they fathomed fully
how far I have traveled,
how so many serpents
stab me with their poison.
My sons' hearts will help them:
they have their mother's lineage.

wrath of Hild: battle

27. We struck with our swords!
Soon my life is ended;
Goinn° scathes me sorely,
settles in my heart's hall°;
I wish the wand of Vidrir°
would wound Ælle, one day.
My sons must feel great fury
that their father is put to death;
my daring swains won't suffer
in silence when they hear this.

Goinn: name of a serpent
heart's hall: chest
Vidrir: Odin; his *wand*: Odin's spear

28. We struck with our swords!
I have stood in the ranks
at fifty one folk-battles,
foremost in the lance-meet.°
Never did I dream that
a different king should ever
be found braver than me—
I bloodied spears when young.
Æsir will ask us to feast;
no anguish for my death.

lance-meet: battle

29. I desire my death now.
The disir[13] call me home,
whom Herjan° hastens onward
from his hall, to take me.
On the high bench, boldly,
beer I'll drink with the Gods;
hope of life is lost now—
laughing shall I die!

Herjan: Odin

BIBLIOGRAPHY

Note that Icelandic authors have been alphabetized by first name, as is common practice.

Acker, Paul. "Introduction to *Skjöldunga saga.*" *ANQ* 20.3 (2007), 3-9

Adam of Bremen. *History of the Archbishops of Hamburg-Bremen.* Trans. Francis J. Tschan. New York: Columbia University Press, 2002.

Annales Fuldenses, sive Annales Regni Francorum Orientalis. Ed. G. H. Pertz. Hanover: Hahn, 1891.

Arnold, Matthew. *Poems: Second Series.* London: Longman, Brown, Green, and Longmans, 1855.

Bachman, W. Bryant and Guðmundur Erlingsson, ed. trans. *The Sagas of King Half and King Hrolf.* Lanham, Md.: University Press of America, 1991.

—, ed. trans. *Six Old Icelandic Sagas.* Lanham, Md.: University Press of America, 1993.

Barnes, Michael P. *The Runic Inscriptions of Maeshowe, Orkney.* Uppsala: Institutionen för nordiska språk, Uppsala universitet, 1994.

Bately, Janet, ed. *The Old English Orosius.* Early English Text Society, Supplementary Series, vol. 6. London: Oxford University Press, 1980.

Bell, R. C. *Board and Table Games from Many Civilizations.* London: Oxford University Press, 1960.

Bjarni Guðnason, ed. *Íslenzk Fornrit XXXV: Danakonunga Sögur.* Reykjavík: Hið

Íslenzka Fornritafélag, 1982.

Bonnetain, Yvonne S. "Potentialities of Loki." *Old Norse Religion in Long-Term Perspectives: Origins, Changes, and Interactions*. Ed. Anders Andrén, Kristina Jennbert, and Catherina Raudvere. Lund: Nordic Academic Press, 2006. 326-330.

Bowles, Adam, ed. trans. *Mahabhárata. Book Eight: Karna, Volume One*. New York: New York University Press / JJC Foundation, 2006.

Byock, Jesse L., ed. trans. *The Saga of the Volsungs*. London: Penguin, 1999.

Cherniak, Alex, ed. trans. *Mahabhárata. Book Six: Bhishma, Volume One*. New York: New York University Press / JJC Foundation, 2008.

Christiansen, Eric, ed. trans. *The Works of Sven Aggesen: Twelfth-Century Danish Historian*. London: Viking Society for Northern Research, 1992.

Clover, Carol J. "Icelandic Family Sagas (*Íslendingasögur*)." *Old Norse–Icelandic Literature: A Critical Guide*. Ed. Carol J. Clover and John Lindow. Toronto: University of Toronto Press / Medieval Academy of America, 2005. 239-315.

Driscoll, M. J. "Traditionality and Antiquarianism in the Post-Reformation *Lygisaga*." *Northern Antiquity: The Post-Medieval Reception of Edda and Saga*. Ed. Andrew Wawn. Enfield Lock: Hisarlik Press, 1994. 83-99

Dumézil, Georges. *The Stakes of the Warrior*. Trans. David Weeks. Berkeley: University of California Press, 1983.

—. *The Destiny of the Warrior*. Trans. Alf Hiltebeitel. Chicago: University of Chicago Press, 1970.

Eiríkr Magnusson and William Morris, trans., Rasmus B. Anderson, ed. *The Völsunga Saga*. London, New York: Norroena Society, 1907.

Finnur Jónsson. *Den Norsk-Islandske Skjaldedigtning*. 4 vols. Copenhagen: Villadsen & Christiansen, 1912-1915.

—. *Ordbog over det Norsk-Islandske Skjaldesprog*. 2nd ed. Copenhagen: S. L. Møller, 1931.

Fjalldal, Magnús. *Anglo-Saxon England in Icelandic Medieval Texts*. Toronto: University of Toronto Press, 2005.

Frank, Roberta. "Skaldic Poetry". *Old Norse–Icelandic Literature: A Critical Guide*. Ed. Carol J. Clover and John Lindow. Toronto: University of Toronto Press / Medieval Academy of America, 2005. 157-196.

Gantz, Jeffrey, ed. *The Mabinogion*. New York: Dorset Press, 1976.

Gelling, Peter and Hilda Roderick Ellis Davidson. *The Chariot of the Sun: and Other Rites and Symbols of the Northern Bronze Age*. New York: Praeger, 1969.

Geoffrey of Monmouth. *The History of the Kings of Britain*. Trans. Lewis G. M. Thorpe. London: Penguin, 1966.

Giles, J. A., ed. *Six Old English Chronicles*. London: Bell & Daldy, 1874.

Grimm, Jakob and Wilhelm Grimm. *The Complete Grimm's Fairy Tales*. Trans. Margaret Hunt. New York: Pantheon, 1944.

Guðbrandur Vigfússon and F. York Powell, eds. *Corpus Poeticum Boreale. Vol. II: Court Poetry*. Oxford: Clarendon Press, 1883.

Guðni Jónsson and Bjarni Vilhjálmson, eds. *Fornaldarsögur Norðurlanda*. 3 vols. Reykjavík: Bókaútgáfan Forni, 1943.

Gunnar Harðarson and Stefán Karlsson. "*Hauksbók.*" *Medieval Scandinavia*. Ed. Phillip Pulsiano and Kirsten Wolf. London: Routledge, 1993. 271-272.

Halldór Hermannsson. *The Saga of Thorgils and Haflidi*. Ithaca, N.Y.: Cornell University Press, 1945.

Hallmundsson, May and Hallberg Hallmundsson, eds. trans. *Icelandic Folk and Fairy Tales*. Reykjavík: Iceland Review, 2005.

Heinrich, Anne. "*Krákumál*". *Medieval Scandinavia*. Ed. Phillip Pulsiano and Kirsten Wolf. London: Routledge, 1993. 368-369.

Bibliography

Hermann Pálsson and Paul Edwards, ed. trans. *The Book of Settlements: Landnámabók*. Winnipeg: University of Manitoba, 1972.

—, ed. trans. *Seven Viking Romances*. London: Penguin, 1985.

Hollander, Lee M., ed. trans. *Jómsvíkinga saga*. Austin: University of Texas Press, 1955.

—, ed. trans. *The Poetic Edda*. 2nd ed. Austin: University of Texas Press, 1962.

Hungerland, Heinz. "Zeugnisse zur Volsungen– und Niflungensage aus der Skaldendichtung (8–16 jh.)" *Arkiv för Nordisk Filologi* 16 (1904): 1-43, 105-141.

Jesch, Judith. *Ships and Men in the Late Viking Age: The Vocabulary of Runic Inscriptions and Skaldic Verse*. Woodbridge, Suffolk: Boydell and Brewer, 2001.

Jochens, Jenny. *Women in Old Norse Society*. Ithaca, N.Y.: Cornell University Press, 1995.

Jones, Gwyn. *A History of the Vikings*. London: Oxford University Press, 1968.

Kalinke, Marianne. "Norse Romance (*Riddarasögur*)." *Old Norse–Icelandic Literature: A Critical Guide*. Ed. Carol J. Clover and John Lindow. Toronto: University of Toronto Press / Medieval Academy of America, 2005. 316-363.

Kennedy, John. "The English Translations of *Völsunga saga*". *Northern Antiquity: The Post-Medieval Reception of Edda and Saga*. Ed. Andrew Wawn. Enfield Lock: Hisarlik Press, 1994. 285-303.

King, David. *Finding Atlantis: A True Story of Genius, Madness, and an Extraordinary Quest for a Lost World*. New York: Harmony Books, 2005.

Krapp, George Philip and Elliott Van Kirk Dobie. *The Anglo-Saxon Poetic Records. Volume III: The Exeter Book*. New York: Columbia University Press, 1936.

Kunin, Devra, ed. *A History of Norway and the Passion and Miracles of the Blessed Óláfr*. London: Viking Society for Northern Research, 2001.

Larson, Laurence, ed. trans. *The Earliest Norwegian Laws: Being the Gulathing Law and the Frostathing Law.* New York: Columbia University Press, 1935.

Lindow, John. "Mythology and Mythography." *Old Norse–Icelandic Literature: A Critical Guide.* Ed. Carol J. Clover and John Lindow. Toronto: University of Toronto Press / Medieval Academy of America, 2005. 21-67.

Mathers, E. P., ed. trans. *The Book of the Thousand Nights and One Night.* Vol. 4. London: Routledge, 1990.

McTurk, Rory. *Studies in* Ragnars saga Loðbrókar *and its Major Scandinavian Analogues.* Medium Ævum Monographs, New Series XV. Oxford: Society for the Study of Mediæval Languages and Literatures, 1991.

—. *"Ragnars saga loðbrókar".* *Medieval Scandinavia.* Ed. Phillip Pulsiano and Kirsten Wolf. London: Routledge, 1993. 519-520.

—. "Kings and Kingship in Viking Northumbria." *Proceedings of the Thirteenth International Saga Conference, Durham and York, 6th-12th August, 2006.* http://www.dur.ac.uk/medieval.www/sagaconf/mcturk.htm Accessed April 19, 2009.

Miller, Clarence H., ed. trans. "Fragments of Danish History". *ANQ* 20.3, 9-22.

Mitchell, Stephen A. *"Fornaldarsögur".* *Medieval Folklore: An Encyclopedia of Myths, Legends, Tales, Beliefs, and Customs.* 2 vols. Ed. Carl Lindahl, John McNamara, and John Lindow. Santa Barbara, Calif.: ABC-CLIO, 2000. 372-374.

Monty Python and the Holy Grail. Dir. Terry Gilliam, Terry Jones. Perf. Graham Chapman, John Cleese, Eric Idle, Terry Gilliam, Terry Jones, Michael Palin. 1975.

Nelson, Janet L., ed. trans. *The Annals of St-Bertin.* Manchester: Manchester University Press, 1991.

Niles, John D., ed. *Beowulf and Lejre.* Tempe, Ariz.: Arizona Center for Medieval and Renaissance Studies, 2007.

O'Connor, Ralph, ed. trans. *Icelandic Histories and Romances.* 2nd ed. Stroud, Gloucestershire: Tempus, 2006.

O'Donohue, Heather. *Old Norse–Icelandic Literature: A Short Introduction.* Oxford: Blackwell, 2004.

—. *From Asgard to Valhalla: The Remarkable History of the Norse Myths.* London: I. B. Tauris, 2007.

Percy, Thomas. *Five Pieces of Runic Poetry: Translated from the Islandic Language.* London: R. and J. Dodsley, 1763.

Pilikian, Vaughan, ed. trans. *Mahabhárata. Book Seven: Drona, Volume One.* New York: New York University Press / JJC Foundation, 2006.

Polomé, Edgar C. "Some Comments on Voluspá, Stanzas 17-18." *Essays on Germanic Religion.* Journal of Indo-European Studies, Monograph Number Six. Washington, DC: Institute for the Study of Man, 1986. 30-54.

Poole, Russell Gilbert. *Viking Poems on War and Peace: A Study in Skaldic Narrative.* Toronto: University of Toronto Press, 1991.

Puhvel, Jaan. *Comparative Mythology.* Baltimore: Johns Hopkins University Press, 1989.

Purcell, Henry. *King Arthur.* [CD recording.] Erato, 1995.

Quinn, Judy. "From Orality to Literacy in Medieval Iceland." *Old Icelandic Literature and Society.* Ed. Margaret Clunies Ross. Cambridge University Press, Cambridge, 2000. 30-60.

Robinson, Charles H. *Anskar, The Apostle of the North, 801-865: Translated from the* Vita Anskarii *by Bishop Rimbert his Fellow Missionary and Sucessor.* London: Society for the Propagation of the Gospel in Foreign Parts, 1921.

Ross, Margaret Clunies. *Prolonged Echoes: Old Norse Myths in Medieval Northern Society. Volume 2: The Reception of Norse Myths in Medieval Iceland.* Odense: Odense University Press, 1998.

Rowe, Elizabeth Ashman. "Helpful Danes and Pagan Irishmen: Saga Fantasies of the Viking Age in the British Isles." *Proceedings of the Thirteenth International Saga Conference, Durham and York, 6th-12th August, 2006.* http://www.dur.ac.uk/

Saxo Grammaticus. *The History of the Danes: Books I-IX*. Ed. Hilda R. Ellis-Davidson, trans. Peter Fisher. Rochester, N.Y.: D.S. Brewer, 1996.

Schlauch, Margaret, ed. trans. *The Saga of the Volsungs; The Saga of Ragnar Lodbrok together with the Lay of Kraka*. New York: W. W. Norton, 1930.

Scholz, Bernhard, ed. trans. *Carolingian Chronicles: Royal Frankish Annals and Nithard's Histories*. Ann Arbor: University of Michigan Press, 1970.

Skre, Dagfinn. "The *Sciringes healh* of Ohthere's Time." *Ohthere's Voyages*. Ed. Janet Bately and Anton Englert. Roskilde: Viking Ship Museum, 2007, 150-155.

Smyth, Alfred P. *Scandinavian Kings in the British Isles, 850-880*. Oxford: Oxford University Press, 1977.

—. "The Effect of Scandinavian Raiders on the English and Irish Churches: A Preliminary Reassessment." *Britain and Ireland, 900-1300: Insular Responses to Medieval European Change*. Ed. Brendan Smith. Cambridge: Cambridge University Press, 1-38.

Snorri Sturluson. *Edda*. Trans. Anthony Faulkes. London: J. M. Dent, 1987.

—. *Heimskringla: History of the Kings of Norway*. Trans. Lee M. Hollander. Austin: University of Texas Press, 1991.

Society for Promoting Christian Knowledge. *Stories of the Norsemen*. London: Society for Promoting Christian Knowledge, 1852.

South, Ted Johnson, ed. trans. *Historia de Sancto Cuthberto*. Cambridge: D. S. Brewer, 2002.

Southey, Robert. "To Amos Cottle." Cottle, A. S. *Icelandic Poetry, or the Edda of Saemund*. Bristol: N. Biggs, 1797. xxxi-xlii.

—. "The Race of Odin." *Joan of Arc, and Minor Poems*. London: George Routledge, 1854. 174-176.

Stevenson, William Henry. *Asser's Life of King Alfred, Together With the Annals of St. Neots Erroneously Ascribed to Asser.* Oxford: Clarendon Press, 1959.

Sweet, Henry. *An Anglo-Saxon Primer: With Grammar, Notes, and Glossary.* 8th ed. Oxford: Clarendon Press, 1896.

Temple, William. *The Works of Sir William Temple, Bart., Complete in Four Volumes.* Volume 3. London: F. C. and J. Rivington, 1814.

Thompson, Stith. *Motif-Index of Folk-Literature.* 5 vols. Bloomington: Indiana University Press, 1973.

Tolkien, Christopher, ed. trans. *The Saga of King Heidrek the Wise.* London: Thomas Nelson and Sons, 1960.

Tolkien, J.R.R. "*Beowulf:* The Monsters and the Critics." *Beowulf: A Verse Translation.* Ed. Daniel Donoghue, trans. Seamus Heaney. Norton Critical Editions. 103-130.

Tulinius, Torfi H. "The Matter of the North: Fiction and Uncertain Identities in Thirteenth-Century Iceland." *Old Icelandic Literature and Society.* Ed. Margaret Clunies Ross. Cambridge University Press, Cambridge, 2000. 242-265.

—. *The Matter of the North: The Rise of Literary Fiction in Thirteenth-Century Iceland.* Odense: Odense University Press, 2002.

Turville-Petre, E. O. G. *Myth and Religion of the North: The Religion of Ancient Scandinavia.* New York: Holt, Rinehart and Winston, 1964.

—. "Dreams in Icelandic Tradition." *Nine Norse Studies.* London: Viking Society for Northern Research, 1972. 30-51.

Turville Petre, Joan, ed. trans. *The Story of Raud and his Sons.* London: Viking Society for Northern Research, 1947.

Uther, Hans-Jörg. *The Types of International Folktales: A Classification and Bibliography Based on the System of Antti Aarne and Stith Thompson. Vols 1–3.* FF Communications No. 284–86, Helsinki: Academia Scientiarum Fennica, 2004.

Valtonas, Irmeli. "Who Were the Cwenas?" *Ohthere's Voyages*. Ed. Janet Bately and Anton Englert. Roskilde: Viking Ship Museum, 2007, 108-109.

Viðar Hreinsson, ed. *Complete Sagas of the Icelanders*. 5 vols. Reykjavík: Leifur Eiriksson Publishing, 1997.

Virgil. *Works. Volume I: Eclogues, Georgics, Aeneid Books I-VI*. Trans. H. Rushton Fairclough, rev. G. P. Goold. Loeb Classical Library. Cambridge, Mass.: Harvard University Press, 1999.

Wawn, Andrew. *The Vikings and the Victorians: Inventing the Old North in 19th-Century Britain*. Cambridge, U.K.: D. S. Brewer, 2000.

Werlauff, Ericus Christianus, ed. *Symbolæ ad Geographiam Medii Ævi, ex Monumentis Islandicis*. Hauniæ [Copenhagen]: Gyldendal, 1821.

Whitelock, Dorothy, ed. trans. *The Anglo-Saxon Chronicle: A Revised Translation*. New Brunswick, N.J.: Rutgers University Press, 1962.

Winn, Shan M. M. *Heaven, Heroes, and Happiness: The Indo-European Roots of Western Ideology*. Lanham, Md.: University Press of America, 1995.

NOTES

All "sagas of Icelanders" cited in the text, whose publication information is not specifically given, may be found in translation in Complete Sagas of Icelanders, edited by Viðar Hreinsson.

Introduction

1   His Norse name Ragnarr Loðbrók is variously anglicized as Ragnar or Regner, and his nickname appears as Lodbrok, Lothbrok, Lodbrog, Lodhbrogh, and so on.
2   Temple, "Of Heroic Virtue", *Works*, vol. 3, p. 368.
3   Purcell, Henry. *King Arthur.* Erato, 1995.
4   Southey, "The Race of Odin", *Joan of Arc*, p. 176.
5   Southey, "To Amos Cottle", in Cottle, *Icelandic Poetry*, pp. xxxiv-xxxv.
6   Wawn, *The Vikings and the Victorians*, pp. 19-23.
7   Arnold, p. 48.
8   Arnold, p. 4.
9   Wawn, pp. 6-7.
10 Wawn, p. 235, n92.
11 See, for example, the Norroena Society's 1907 edition of Magnusson and Morris's translation of *Völsunga saga*.
12 See O'Donoghue, *From Asgard to Valhalla*, for more discussion of the survival of Norse myth and legend in modern culture.
13 Saxo Grammaticus, *History of the Danes* Preface.5, trans. Ellis-Davidson and Fisher, p. 5.
14 Material concerning Ragnar and his family also appears in Danish, Norwegian, and Faroese ballads. Rory McTurk's *Studies in* Ragnars saga Loðbrókar collates all variants of Ragnar's legend, in much more detail than I can give here.
15 Thomas Love Peacock; quoted in Frank, "Skaldic Poetry", p. 160.
16 Adam of Bremen, *History of the Archbishops of Hamburg Bremen* IV.xxxvi, Scholium 156; Tschan, trans., p. 217.

17 Some scholars subdivide the *fornaldarsögur* into "heroic sagas", which feature a legendary hero's deeds and death and which often have links with other old Germanic texts such as *Beowulf* or the Nibelungenlied; "Viking sagas", which allegedly take place in historic times; and "adventure tales", which usually end happily ever after, taking place in a sort of legendary Neverland.

18 Driscoll, "Post-Reformation *Lygisaga*", pp. 83-99.

19 King, *Finding Atlantis*, pp. 29-39.

20 Kalinké, "Norse Romance", pp. 324-328.

21 *Völsunga saga* ch. 23; trans. Byock, pp. 72-73.

22 *Óláfs saga Tryggvasonar* ch. 64; Hollander, trans., pp. 203-204.

23 Clover, "Icelandic Family Sagas", p. 245

24 Tulinius, "The Matter of the North", pp. 248-249.

25 Tulinius, *The Matter of the North*.

26 Ross, *Prolonged Echoes*, vol. 2, pp. 50 51; O'Connor, *Icelandic Histories and Romances*, pp. 41-46.

27 My translation from the text in *Fornaldarsögur Norðurlanda* vol. 3, pp. 393-394.

28 My translation from the text in *Fornaldarsögur Norðurlanda* vol. 2, p. 436.

29 My translation from the text in *Fornaldarsögur Norðurlanda* vol. 2, p. 359.

30 My translation from the text in Hermannson, *Saga of Thorgils and Haflidi*, p. 14.

31 *Fornaldarsögur Norðurlanda* vol. 2, pp. 271-286. Translated in Bachman and Erlingsson, *Six Old Icelandic Sagas*, pp. 1-13.

32 Chs. 6-9; trans. Pálsson and Edwards, pp. 18-22.

33 See e.g. Quinn, "From Orality to Literacy", pp. 46-51, and Ross, *Prolonged Echoes*, vol. 2, pp. 76-96, for a discussion of the role of genealogies as a framework for Icelandic literary works.

34 *Landnámabók*, ch. 208; Pálsson and Edwards, trans., pp. 93-94.

35 *Landnámabók*, ch. 177; Pálsson and Edwards, trans., p. 82.

36 Ross, *Prolonged Echoes*, vol. 2, p. 92.

37 Quoted in Mitchell, "*Fornaldarsögur*", p. 374.

38 Tolkien, "*Beowulf*: The Monsters and the Critics", p. 105.

39 Tolkien, p. 127.

40 Ch. 11; trans. Tolkien, *Saga of King Heidrek*, p. 60.

41 Ch. 9; trans. Pálsson and Edwards, *Seven Viking Romances*, pp. 214-215.

42 *History of the Danes* VIII.263, p. 243.

43 Guðnason, ed. *Danakonunga sögur*, p. 326.

44 Scholz, *Carolingian Chronicles*, p. 94.

45 Smyth, *Scandinavian Kings*, pp. 1-6.

46 *History of the Danes* VIII.262, pp. 241-242.

47 Puhvel, *Comparative Mythology*, p. 285; Winn, *Heaven, Heroes, and Happiness*, pp. 209-234.

48 Dumézil, *The Stakes of the Warrior*, pp. 71-78.

49 *Mahabhárata: Bhisma* 56.1-2, 10-11; trans. Cherniak, pp. 472-473. See also, e.g., *Mahabhátara: Karna* 11.13-15, 11-28; trans. Bowles, pp. 130-133.

50 *Mahabhárata: Drona* 7.32-7.42; trans. Pilikian, pp. 72-73.

51 Lindow, "Mythology and Mythography", pp. 45-46.

52 *Völsunga saga* ch. 1; trans. Byock, p. 36

53 *History of the Danes* VII.248-249, pp. 226-227.

54 *History of the Danes* I.32, p. 31.

55 *Reginsmál* 23; trans. Hollander, *Poetic Edda*, p. 222.

56 *Ynglinga saga* ch. 7; trans. Hollander, *Heimskringla*, p. 11.

57 In *Hákonar saga gamla* ch. 162; quoted in Guðnasson, *Danakonunga sögur*, p. 60 n28.

58 *Destiny of the Warrior* pp. 90-95.

59 Chs. 3-7; trans. Pálsson and Edwards, *Seven Viking Romances*, pp. 145-159.

60 *Stakes of the Warrior*, pp. 38-49.

61 e.g. Turville-Petre, *Myth and Religion of the North*, pp. 118-119; Bonnetain, "Potentialities of Loki", p. 327.

62 McTurk, *Studies in* Ragnars saga, pp. 1-6.

63 e.g. *Annals of St-Bertin*, trans. Nelson, pp. 61-62

64 Smyth, *Scandinavian Kings*, pp. 86-100.

65 *History of the Archbishops of Hamburg-Bremen* I.xxxvii; trans. Tschan, p. 37

66 *Anglo-Saxon Chronicle* p. 46 n6. Ivar's name is variously spelled variously spelled Ingware, Hingwar, and so on; Ubbi appears as Ubba, Hubba, Hubbi, etc.

67 *De Rebus Gestis Alfredi* 54b; ed. Stevenson, *Asser's Life of King Alfred*, p. 44.

68 Jones, *History of the Vikings*, pp. 215-218

69 McTurk, *Studies in* Ragnars saga, pp. 40-45.

70 McTurk, *Studies in* Ragnars saga, pp. 41-45.

71 McTurk, *Studies in* Ragnars saga, pp. 12-13.

72 Thompson, *Motif-Index of Folk-Literature*, types H1054, H1061, H1063.

73 Aarne-Thompson type 510; see Uther, *Types of International Folktales*.

74 McTurk, *Studies in* Ragnars saga, pp. 1-50. Note that in the best manuscript of Ragnars saga, NkS 1824, the closing poem mentions *synir lodbroku*, "sons of Loðbrók", with the name inflected as if it were a feminine noun.

75 Edgar Polomé connected Loðkona with the mysterious god *Lóðurr*, whose name he interpreted as "man of growth", mentioned only in two verses of the *Völuspá* in the *Poetic Edda*. He identified them both as gods of fertility and abundance. See "Some Comments on Voluspá", pp. 30-54.

76 Barnes, *Runic Inscriptions of Maeshowe*, pp. 178-186.

77 Rowe, "Helpful Danes and Pagan Irishmen".

78 Ch. 4; Hollander, trans., p. 39.

79 For a brief discussion and extensive bibliography, see McTurk, *"Ragnars saga loðbrókar"*, pp. 519-520.

80 Schlauch, *The Saga of the Volsungs*, pp. 183-256.

81 For a translation of *Rerum Danicarum fragmenta* see Miller, "Fragments of Danish History", pp. 9-22.

82 Acker, "Fragments of Danish History", pp. 3-4.

83 McTurk, p. 56.

84 Harðarson and Karlson, *"Hauksbók"*, pp. 271-272.

85 Heinrich, *"Krákumál"*, pp. 368-369.

86 Smith, *Scandinavian Kings*, pp. 73-82.

87 Kennedy, "English Translations", pp. 285-303.

88 http://www.turbidwater.com/portfolio/downloads/RagnarsSaga.pdf

89 http://www.oe.eclipse.co.uk/nom/Ragnar%27s%20Sons.htm

Saga of Ragnar Lodbrok and his Sons

1 *Völsunga saga* (chs. 24-25, 29; trans. Byock, pp. 75-82) introduces Heimir as the husband of Brynhild's sister Bekkhild, as well as both Brynhild's and Aslaug's foster-father.

2 A harp big enough to conceal a person appears in *Bósa saga ok Herrauðs* chs. 12-13 (trans. Pálsson and Edwards, *Seven Viking Romances*, pp. 220-221). The motif may have been borrowed from the Tristan legend (McTurk, *Studies in* Ragnars saga, pp. 236-237)

3 *Vínlaukr* means "wine leek", although *laukr* could also be applied to onions or garlic. In modern Norwegian, *vinlauk* means the purple-flowered onion (*Allium atropurpureum*), which is edible, but usually grown as an ornamental today.

4 Located near Lindesnes, the southernmost point of Norway. *Spangareið* means "Spangle Isthmus" or "Spangle Neck".

5 *Kráka* means "crow".

6 *Bósa saga ok Herrauðs* (ch. 16; trans. Pálsson and Edwards, *Seven Viking Romances*, p. 227) claims that this snake hatched from an egg that Herraud and his friend Bosi brought back from plundering an evil temple in Bjarmaland, north of Russia. Saxo just says that Herraud's friends found some little snakes while hunting, and that Herraud gave them to his daughter, who ended up with two giant snakes, not just one. (*History of the Danes* IX.302, p. 281)

7 An Icelandic folktale tells of a girl who is given a gold ring and puts it under

a "ling snake" in her linen chest; the snake and the gold beneath it both grow, until the girl throws the chest in a lake, where the snake is said to still live on the huge but unattainable treasure. ("Ormurinn í Lagarfljóti", *Íslenzkar Þjóðsögur og Æfintýri* vol. 1, p. 635; trans. Hallmundsson and Hallmundsson, "The Serpent of Lagarfljót", *Icelandic Folk and Fairy Tales*, pp. 96-97.)

8   Both the *Sögubrot* and *Hervarar saga* (ch. 11; trans. Tolkien, *Saga of King Heidrek*, pp. 59-60) describe this deed; however, Saxo makes Regner's father Ring a distant descendant of the King Ring who fought at Brávellir.

9   As Saxo tells it, he soaks his shaggy woolen clothes in cold water, which freezes into a protective layer of ice. (*History of the Danes* IX.302, p. 281)

10 The motif of identifying a dragon's killer by part of the weapon left sticking in the corpse may be derived from the Tristan legend, via the Norse *Tristrams saga ok Ísöndar* (McTurk, *Studies in* Ragnars saga, pp. 235-239)

11 In the sagas in general, extremely long, flowing, fair hair is the hallmark of an exceptionally beautiful woman (e.g. *Gunnlaugs saga ormstungu* ch. 4; *Njáls saga* ch. 13, 33).

12 It's a fairly common folktale motif for a would-be royal bride to have to solve "oppositional paradoxes" like these (motifs H1050–H1064 in Thompson, *Motif-Index of Folk-Literature*). For example, see Grimm's "The Peasant's Clever Daughter" (Tale #94 in *The Complete Grimm's Fairy Tales*, pp. 437-440; or "The Chick-Pea Seller's Daughter" in the *Arabian Nights* (*The Book of the Thousand Nights and One Night*, Mathers, ed. trans., pp. 210-214).

13 Tulinius points out a similarity with the legend of St. Agnes, known in medieval Iceland as *Agnesar saga*. When Agnes refuses to marry a pagan who loves her, he becomes furious and strips off her clothes; however, Agnes's hair miraculously grows long and covers her, thus saving her modesty. (*Matter of the North*, pp. 132-135)

14 In the Faeroese ballad *Ragnars kvæði*, Thora prophesies before she dies that her clothes will fit Ragnar's next wife perfectly, which is how he will be able to recognize her (McTurk, *Studies in* Ragnars saga, p. 191).

15 The phrase *drykkja brúðlaup* literally means "to drink the wedding", which reflects how much drinking was a part of social rites. See Jochens, *Women in Old Norse Society*, pp. 105-111 for a discussion of Old Norse drinking culture.

16 Aslaug's desire to wait to consummate her marriage for three nights may ultimately derive from the Vulgate translation of Tobit 8:4 in the Biblical Apocrypha, in which Tobias and Sara spend their first three wedded nights in prayer (a custom known in medieval times as the "nights of Tobias"). In both the Frankish *Chronicle of Fredegarius* and in *Jómsvíkinga saga*, a newly married couple abstains from sex in order to have prophetic dreams of their descendants'

fates; there is also the episode in *Völsunga saga* (ch. 29; trans. Byock, p. 81) in which Sigurd, disguised as Gunnar, spends three chaste wedding nights beside Brynhild, claiming that he is fated to die unless he does so. Any or all of these sources could have contributed to this episode (McTurk, *Studies in* Ragnars saga, pp. 93-96).

17 The pagan ceremony of naming a child included sprinkling the child with water, *vatni ausa* (see, for example, *Egils saga* chs. 31, 35).

18 It's been speculated that Ivar had the hereditary bone disease *osteogenesis imperfecta*, or "brittle-bone disease". Others have suggested that "boneless" originally meant "impotent", which could be confirmed by the statement in Chapter IV of the *Tale of Ragnar's Sons* that Ivar "had no lust nor love in him". The name could be a different metaphor: since *beinn* can mean "leg" and snakes have no legs, Ivar's nickname might have meant "Ivar the Serpent". "Boneless" is a term for the wind in Norwegian folk tradition, which might make Ivar's name imply something like "the Sailor by the Wind" or "the Navigator". Finally, it's been proposed that the name resulted from a misreading of a Latin source, reading *exos* (boneless) for *exosus* (hateful). (McTurk, "Kings and Kingship in Viking Northumbria", p. 4)

19 *Hvítabær* means "white settlement". Assuming that the Hvítabær in this saga can be identified with any real-world location, it might be Whitby, on the coast of Northumbria in England (which was in fact attacked by Vikings in 867), or Vitaby, in Skåne in present-day southernmost Sweden.

20 The Old Norse is *blótskapr*, literally meaning "sacrifices", but connoting some sort of hostile magic worked by means of heathen sacrifice. There is no simple English equivalent.

21 Again hard to translate: *tröllskapr* is literally "the state of being a troll" but usually means some sort of hostile magical power. *Tröll* can refer to a wide range of uncanny beings, not necessarily human in shape, but usually hostile.

22 Cows that have become supernaturally powerful from being worshipped appear not only in this saga; a man-eating *blótnaut* (sacrifice-bull) whose bellowing is terrifying appears in *Hjálmpés saga ok Ölvis* (ch. 10; trans. O'Connor, *Icelandic Histories and Romances*, p. 157). *Óláfs saga Tryggvasonar* (ch. 64; trans. Hollander, *Heimskringla*, pp. 203-204) mentions an ancient king who worshipped a cow and drank her milk. There is also Auðumla, the cow whose milk nourishes Ymir, the primordial being, in Norse cosmology. Given the many Bronze Age rock carvings of cows, some of which might include ritual scenes (Gelling and Ellis-Davidson, *Chariot of the Sun*, pp. 81-85, figs. 37-41, pp. 163-164), it's just possible, if speculative, that these texts could preserve some garbled memory of a tradition of sacred cattle.

23 According to *Hervarar saga* ch. 11 (trans. Tolkien, *Saga of King Heidrek*, p. 60), this Eystein was a son of Harald Wartooth, and was also known as *Eysteinn inn illráði*, "Eystein the Wicked" or "Eystein the Bad Ruler".

24 The name *Síbilja* is probably not derived from the Latin Sybil, despite the similarity. McTurk (*Studies in* Ragnars saga, pp. 114-116) has proposed that the name Sibilja is cognate with the Sanskrit name *Savala*, "pied; mottled", applied to a "cow of plenty" in the *Ramayana* and other Indian myths. The name might have been learned by early medieval Germanic peoples from Indo-Iranian language speakers such as the Alans.

25 Tulinius points out that medieval Icelandic women ran the risk of being given up as wives or concubines, if their men wanted to marry higher-ranking spouses. The story of how Aslaug manages to stop this from happening to her is unusual in Norse literature, and may have resonated strongly with women who heard the saga. (*Matter of the North*, pp. 130-135)

26 Another motif from the Volsung legend, in which Sigurd gains the ability to understand the speech of birds. (*Völsunga saga* chs. 19-20, 23; Byock, trans., pp. 65-66, 72)

27 Saxo gives a very different story: Odin, disguised as an old man named Roftar (Old Norse *Hroptr*), healed Sigurd of a festering wound. In exchange, Sigurd dedicated all those he killed in battle to Odin. Odin sprinkled dust in Sigurd's eyes, which left the snake-like markings that gave him his nickname. (*History of the Danes* IX.304, p. 283)

28 More is at stake here than meets the eye. In Norse society, a newborn child was ritually carried to the putative father for him to formally accept as his own, and to name. If the father rejected the child, it could be left outside to die of exposure. (Jochens, *Women in Old Norse Society*, pp. 83-94) By naming the child, Ragnar breaks the dramatic tension that has been building up, acknowledging both his fatherhood and the truth of Aslaug's claims.

29 When someone was given a name—even when a grown man was dubbed with a nickname—the one who gave the name traditionally gave a gift along with it, a *nafnfestr* ("name-fastening").

30 "To hate gold" is a common poetic expression for great generosity—someone who is always freely giving away gold may metaphorically be said to "hate" it.

31 "To fare over a land with war-shields" (*fara yfir land herskildi*) means "to raid; to devastate". *Eiríks saga rauða* (chs. 10-11) mentions red shields used by a hostile force, while white shields were a token of peace.

32 An arrow that was passed from household to household as a summons to military action. The custom is mentioned in both legal codes (e.g. *Gulaþingslög*, chs. 151, 160, trans. Larson, *The Earliest Norwegian Laws*, pp. 128, 132) and in

sagas (e.g. *Óláfs sags Tryggvasonar* chs. 17, 40, 53, 65, etc).

33 "To buy a maiden with rings" means to pay a bride-price, one of several financial transactions that accompanied any marriage. There is a parallel passage in the Old English poem *Maxims I*, 81-82: *Cyning sceal mid ceape cwene gebicgan, bunum ond beagum*, "A king must buy a woman with a price, with cups and rings." (Krapp and Dobie, *Anglo-Saxon Poetic Records*, vol. 3, p. 159)

34 Some versions of these verses give this line as *ef svá duga dísir*, "if the *dísir* aid us" (Vigfússon and Powell, *Corpus Poeticum Boreale*, vol. II, p. 349). The *dísir* are protective female spirits associated with a family line; see note 13 to *Krákumál*.

35 The motif of the precocious, warlike three-year-old boy who can compose skaldic poetic stanzas appears in *Egils saga* (ch. 31).

36 The line *at hváriga nytak* literally means, and is usually translated, "though I can use neither." But *hvárigr*, confusingly, can also mean "either one", and we've already seen that Ivar is a mighty archer who can definitely use both arms. I've chosen this translation for the sake of dramatic consistency.

37 Possibly derived from *randa-Hlín*, "shield-goddess"; McTurk, *Studies in* Ragnars saga, p. 178.

38 Identified as Wiflisburg, the German name for Avenches in present-day Switzerland. According to the Icelander Abbot Nicholas of Þverá, whose *Leiðarvísir* describes the pilgrimage route from Scandinavia to Jerusalem, several sites on the route were identified with the legends of Sigurd and Ragnar. These included the heath where Sigurd killed Fafnir, said to be between Paderborn and Mainz; Vifilsborg, said to have been a great city before Ragnar's sons destroyed it; and Luna in Italy. (McTurk, *Studies in* Ragnars saga, pp. 109-110; Werlauff, *Symbolae*, pp. 16-20)

39 Now Luni, a town on the northwest coast of Italy, near Genoa. Besides its mention in the sagas of Ragnar, Nicholas of Þverá claimed that the sands near Luna were the site of the snakepit where Gunnar was killed (Werlauff, *Symbolae*, p. 20). According to Dudo of St. Quentin, Luna was sacked in 860 by Bjorn's and Hastein's forces; the attackers allegedly thought Luna was Rome. (Jones, *History of the Vikings*, pp. 217-8) Other chronicles mention raids in 860 on towns in northern Italy, carried out by Vikings based in the Rhône delta in the south of France (e.g. Nelson, *Annals of St-Bertin*, p. 93).

40 Wearing out iron shoes on a long journey is a fairly common folktale motif (H1125, Q502.2, in Thompson, *Motif-Index of Folk-Literature*). But the idea of discouraging invaders by showing them shoes that have (allegedly) been worn out on the journey may have Biblical roots, in the tale of the "Gibeonite deception" (Joshua 9:1-15). A version of the story appears in *Norna-Gests þáttr* ch. 9 (*Fornaldarsögur Norðurlanda* vol. 1, pp. 184-185), in which the old man is

interpreted as a spirit sent by God to save Rome from pillage.

41 The Old Norse word *knörr* can simply mean "ship", but by the 11ᵗʰ century the word had taken on the specific meaning of a large, broad class of ship, used as both commercial and military transports. The Anglo-Saxon poem *The Battle of Brunanburh* mentions invading Vikings using a *knörr* (Old English *cnear*) in 937, so the idea of Ragnar raiding England with two *knerrir* is at least historically plausible (Jesch, *Ships and Men*, pp. 128-132).

42 According to the *Anglo-Saxon Chronicle*, the Great Heathen Army, led by the alleged sons of Ragnar, invaded East Anglia in the year 866 and moved into Northumbria in 867. That year, there was a civil war in Northumbria, because Ælle had taken the throne from the hereditary king Osberht. Ælle and Osberht settled their differences and raised an army together, but both kings were killed in the ensuing battle. There is no record of Ragnar leading an earlier expedition against Ælle; since Ælle was king for less than one year, there would be little time for that to have happened.

43 The text reads *hnefatafl*, a board game superficially similar to chess, and a common pastime of nobles, heroes, and even the gods (according to *Völuspá* 8, 60; trans. Hollander, *Poetic Edda*, pp. 3, 12). See Bell, *Board and Table Games*, pp. 77-81, for a reconstruction of the rules.

44 There may be an untranslatable pun here. The text reads *oss sé mislagðar hendr í kné*, "that we have mislaid hands on the knee". "To mislay one's hands" means to do the wrong thing, but retainers and supplicants of kings traditionally knelt before them and laid their hands on the king's knee; see the Old English poem *The Wanderer* 41-44 (Krapp and Dobie, *Anglo-Saxon Poetic Records*, vol. 3, p. 135).

45 In the *Þáttr af Ragnars sonum*, Ivar founds York in this way. Neither story is remotely true, as both London and York predate the Vikings by centuries. Ivar's scheme was probably borrowed from the *Aeneid* (I.365-368; trans. Fairclough, *Virgil*, pp. 286-287), in which Dido wins the land where Carthage will be built by stretching a bull's hide thong around a hill; or from Geoffrey of Monmouth's *History of the Kings of Britain* (VI.12; trans. Thorpe, pp. 158-159), in which Hengist wins the land for his fort from Vortigern in the same way. That said, the theme of someone founding a realm by asking for what the giver thinks will be a tiny piece of land, and then reinterpreting the terms so as to get a large piece, is known in Norse mythology; compare Gefjon plowing up Zealand in Snorri's *Edda* (*Gylfaginning* 1; Faulkes, trans., p. 7).

46 As explained more fully in the notes to the *Tale of Ragnar's Sons*, this event may derive from a misunderstanding of skaldic poetry, in which the expression "carved by an eagle" (i.e. scavenged) could be interpreted as "carved with an

eagle". See Frank, "Skaldic Poetry", pp. 170-172.

47 In Saxo's telling (*History of the Danes* IX.311, pp. 288-289), Hvitserk is ruling Scythia when he is captured by Daxon, the king of the Ruthenians (Ukrainians), who grants his request to be burned on a pyre. But Saxo places the episode before Ragnar's death, and has Ragnar avenge Hvitserk.

48 Also known as Harald Hardrada (*Haraldr harðráði*), who invaded England and was killed with most of his army at the Battle of Stamford Bridge on September 25, 1066.

49 "William the Bastard" is better known as William the Conqueror, whose invasion of England succeeded at the Battle of Hastings on October 14, 1066.

50 This motif could be derived from Celtic lore; compare the story of the head of Bran the Blessed, which protected Britain from plague as long as it was buried in London (see "Branwen the Daughter of Llyr" in Gantz, trans., *Mabinogion*, pp. 79-81).

51 Thord is mentioned in *Landnámabók* (S208; trans. Pálsson and Edwards, pp. 93-94), which calls him Bjorn's great-grandson and the founder of a very large and prominent family (his descendants included both Snorri Sturluson and Thorfinn Karlsefni, who led the expedition to settle Vinland).

52 *drekka erfi*, "to drink the inheritance", refers to a ritual in which the heir of a deceased man is rightfully confirmed in his inheritance. A description of the rite appears in *Ynglinga saga* ch. 36 (trans. Hollander, trans., *Heimskringla*, p. 39); see also Jochens, *Women in Old Norse Society*, p. 106.

53 "Sun-seeking bitch" refers to the myth that a wolf chases the sun and will some day catch and swallow it; see *Gylfaginning* 12 (trans. Faulkes, *Edda*, pp. 14-15), *Grímnismál* 40 (trans. Hollander, *Poetic Edda*, p. 61).

54 An almost identical stanza appears in *Hálfs saga ok hálfsrekka* ch. 2 (in *Fornaldarsögur Norðurlanda* vol. 2, p. 160; trans. Bachman, *Sagas of King Half and King Hrolf*), where it is spoken by a dead king in a mound. Poole (*Viking Poems*, pp. 20-22) has argued convincingly that the stanza was borrowed into *Hálfs saga* from *Ragnars saga*, and also points out influence from stanzas 49 and 50 of the *Hávamál* in the *Poetic Edda*.

Sögubrot

1 She's not the same as the famous Aud the Deep-Minded who led her family to settle in Iceland; her story appears in *Landnámabók* and *Laxdæla saga*.

2 In the original text, Aud's name varies between Auðr and Unnr, sometimes changing from one paragraph to the next. I have changed all occurrences of her name to Aud for the sake of consistency.

3   *Njáls saga* ch. 25, *Hversu Nóregr byggðist* chs. 3, 5 (*Fornaldarsögur Norðurlanda* vol. 2 pp. 143-145) and *Hyndluljóð* 28 in the *Poetic Edda* (trans. Hollander, p. 135), give the same genealogy as the *Sögubrot*, but call Hrærek *slöngvanbaugi*, "Ring-Slinger", presumably for his great generosity. *Sögubrot* ch. 6 (below) says that it was Harald's son, not his father, who was known as Hrærek *slöngvanbaugi*. *Hervarar saga* (ch. 11; trans. Tolkien, *Saga of King Heidrek*, p. 59) agrees that Harald was Ivar's grandson, but says that Haraldr was the son of Valdar, a petty king whom Ivar set over Denmark, and Ivar's daughter Alfhild. Saxo gives a quite different lineage, making Harald to be the son of the hero Haldan and Gurith, the last female of the old royal line of Denmark (*History of the Danes* VII.239-247, pp. 219-225).

4   Saxo claims that Harald got his name either because he had prominent teeth, or because two of his teeth were knocked out in a fight but unexpectedly grew back (*History of the Danes* VII.247, p. 226).

5   Several other texts mention that one who sleeps in a new bed will have prophetic dreams. Often the bed must be in a room or even a house where no one has ever slept (e.g. Turville-Petre, trans., *Story of Rauð*, p. 19; Hollander, trans., *Jómsvíkinga saga* ch. 2, pp. 31-34).

6   "Fetch" is the equivalent in English folklore of Old Norse *fylgja* (literally "follower"), a guardian spirit attached to each human. It is rarely seen in waking life except by people with second sight, or people on the point of death, but it often appears in dreams. It frequently takes the form of an animal whose nature is like the person's; kings generally have particularly noble or powerful animals as *fylgjur*. (Turville-Petre, "Dreams in Icelandic Tradition", pp. 36-39)

7   Norse kings spent part of the year traveling to each of their major retainers in turn, who were obliged to feast and entertain them. See Note 18 below.

8   Old Norse *Garðaríki*, "Kingdom of Towns"; the usual Norse word for Russia.

9   Probably the present-day Gulf of Finland in the Baltic Sea.

10   The word *lypting* appears to mean a raised, enclosed place on the afterdeck of a ship, sometimes translated "poop-deck". However, no such structure has yet been found on the remains of any Viking-era ship. (Jesch, *Ships and Men*, p. 153)

11   Heimdall is called *heimskr*, "foolish" or "stupid", but the word is related to *heimr*, "home"—etymologically, *heimskr* means "stay-at-home". Heimdallr is taunted with this in *Lokasenna* 48 in the *Poetic Edda* (trans. Hollander, p. 100); as the watchman of the gods, he has to stay at home on guard duty, instead of getting out and about the way that, say, Odin and Loki do.

12   The word used here is *seiðr*, whose nature is not certain. In several sagas, *seiðr* is used to foretell the future, but it could also be used to injure or confuse

people. *Ynglinga saga* ch. 7 (*Heimskringla*, trans. Hollander, p. 11) claims that *seiðr* is unmanly and unfit for men to practice—but at least in this saga, it does Harald no discredit to be protected by it.

13 Granmar and his son-in-law Hervard or Hjorvard, the rulers of what is now Södermanland in southern Sweden, were burned to death in their hall by their adversary, king Ingjald Bad-Ruler. (*Ynglinga saga* chs. 37-39, in *Heimskringla*, trans. Hollander, pp. 40-43)

14 This specific king doesn't seem to appear in any other sources, but the names Hildibrand and Hildir occur in genealogies of the family of the Hildings, descended from Halfdan the Old (see note 32 to the *Tale of Ragnar's Sons*). A famous warrior named Hildibrand also appears in the Old High German *Hildebrandslied* and in the Old Norse *Þiðrekssaga* and *Ásmundar saga kappabana*, but his deeds appear to have nothing in common with Hildibrand in the *Sögubrot*.

15 A ritual drinking-feast in which the heir would formally be seated in his father's high seat and claim his inheritance; described in *Ynglinga saga* ch. 36 (*Heimskringla*, trans. Hollander, p. 39).

16 In the manuscript, this chapter is named *Um kapp Hildar*, "About the Eagerness of Hild" or "About the Conflict of Hild", which is the only clue to what happens next. (Guðnasson, *Danakonunga sögur*, p. 58 n24)

17 According to the *Sögubrot* and also *Hversu Nóregr byggðist* (chs. 3, 5; *Fornaldarsögur Norðurlanda* vol. 2, pp. 140-144), Aud and Hrærek were the parents of Harald Wartooth, whereas Aud and Radbard were the parents of Randver, who was the father of Sigurd Hring. *History of the Danes*, however, makes Hring to be the son of Ingeld, who kidnapped and married Harald's sister.

18 *yfirsókn* literally means "a survey; an overview." Here it refers to the right and custom of a king to move his court from place to place within his lands, staying with each of his vassals in turn and being feasted for a legally specified length of time. This is more usually called *veizla*.

19 Note that the *List of Swedish Kings*, and also *Hversu Nóregr byggðist* (ch. 3; *Fornaldarsögur Norðurlanda* vol. 2, pp.144-145), make Alfhild the great-granddaughter of King Alf.

20 *Elfr* is a Norse word meaning "river", cognate with Swedish *älv* and the German name *Elbe*, going back to Proto-Germanic **albiz*. The writer is interpreting Alfheim as "river-home", located between the Gautelfr (now the Göta älv) and Raumelfr (now the Glomma or Glåma River), and thus roughly equal to the Swedish province of Bohuslän. *Ynglinga saga* (ch. 48; *Heimskringla*, trans. Hollander, p. 48) and *Hversu Nóregr byggðist* (ch. 1; *Fornaldarsögur Norðurlanda* vol. 2, pp. 137-140) tell the same story. However, the tradition that the folk of Alfheim were unusually beautiful is mentioned in chapter 10 of the *Sögubrot* and in a

few legendary sagas, such as one version of *Hervarar saga* (*Saga of King Heidrek*, trans. Tolkien, p. 67). *Hversu Nóregr byggðist* (ch. 1; *Fornaldarsögur Norðurlanda*, vol. 2, p. 140) adds that Alf the king of Alfheim married Svanhildr *gullfjöðr* (Gold-feather), the daughter of Dagr (Day), the son of Delling (Daybreak) and Sól (Sun). This saga thus preserves traditions about the mythological beings known as the *álfar* or elves, who are associated with the sun—e.g. the poetic name *álfröðull*, "alf-beam", for the sun in *Vafþrúðnismál* 47 and *Skírnismál* 4 (*Poetic Edda*, trans. Hollander, pp. 50, 66), and the kenning *Álfheims blika*, "gleam of Alfheim", quoted in *Skaldskaparmál* 18 (*Edda*, trans. Faulkes, p. 86).

21 This is, of course, Ragnarr Loðbrók ("Hairy-Breeches"). Saxo inserts a few generations between the Hring who fought at Brávellir and his descendant Sigurd Ring who fathers Ragnar.

22 As stated in note 3 above, other sources say that it was Harald's father Hrærek who was known as "Ring-Slinger". Saxo mentions a much older king Rørik Slyngebond, i.e. Hrærek *slöngvanbaugi*; this king earned the nickname in a somewhat less exalted fashion. (*History of the Danes* III.85, p. 81)

23 Thrand the Old was said to be the ancestor of prominent Icelanders, including Snorri Sturluson's family, the Oddaverjar (*Njáls saga* ch. 25); however, *Landnámabók* (*Sturlubók* 338, trans. Pálsson and Edwards, p. 128) claims that Thrand's brother Hraerek Ring-Slinger was the ancestor of the Oddaverjar. According to *Hervarar saga* ch. 11 (trans. Tolkien, p. 60), Harald Wartooth had another son named *Eysteinn inn illráði*, "Eystein Bad-Ruler", who ruled Sweden until he was killed by the sons of Ragnar.

24 Probably near the site of present-day Stockholm.

25 This is the sound between Zealand (Denmark) and the Swedish mainland. But the geography seems confused; the Kolmerk forest (now Kolmården) and Brávík (Bråviken, near the modern Swedish city of Nörrkoping) are east of the Øresund. The word *vestr* (west; westwards) might be an error for *vestan* (from the west).

26 The text reads *Kænagarð*, "city of the *Kænir*". *Kænir* seems to be an alternate spelling for *Kvenir*, "Kvens", a Finnic-speaking people known as *Kainu* in Finnish sources, living around the northern shores of the Gulf of Bothnia. (Valtonas, "Who Were the Cwenas", pp. 108-109)

27 Marking the boundaries of a battlefield with stakes of hazel wood was part of the ritual of *hólmganga*, judicial single combat (e.g. *Kormaks saga* ch. 10). Here, and in some other sagas, it is done before a battle between armies (*Hervarar saga* ch. 10; *Egils saga* ch. 52; *Hákonar saga góða* ch. 24 and *Ólafs saga Tryggvasonar* ch. 18, in *Heimskringla*).

28 In Saxo's *History*, Bruni is explicitly said to be Odin in disguise. The *Sögubrot*

never says this directly.

29   These lists of heroes either alliterate according to the rules of Norse poetry, or could be made to alliterate with a slight rearrangement. It's likely that this section is based on a poetic list, or *þulr*; Saxo's list of the fighters is close enough to this text that it was probably based on the same *þulr*.

30   Visina and Heid are mentioned in Saxo (VIII.258, pp. 238-239) and also in the Latin *Chronicon Lethrense* (ch. 9; trans. Newlands, in Niles, *Beowulf and Lejre*, p. 327). Both state that Heid survived the battle and ruled Denmark for a while with Hring's permission; the *Chronicon Lethrense* claims (probably inaccurately) that she founded the trading town of Hedeby.

31   Saxo tells how Harald captured Ubbi by having his men grapple with him, since weapons had no effect on him. Harald later befriended him and gave him his daughter in marriage. Several other of Harald's champions listed here are also said to be his former enemies. (*History of the Danes* VI.249-250, pp. 227-228). The English saint's life *Historia de sancto Cuthberto* (ch. 10; trans. South, pp. 49-50) claims that the great invasion of England in 867 was led by *Ubba dux Frescionum*, "Ubba Duke of the Frisians", rather than by Ivar the son of Ragnar Lodbrok. There may be some conflation here between Ubbi the illegitimate son of Ragnar, who is not mentioned in the Norse sagas but is attested in Saxo, and the hero Ubbi the Frisian.

32   The Wends (Vindir) were eastern Slavs, who at the time lived along the south Baltic coast just east of Denmark.

33   The *svínfylkja* or "swine formation" refers to the wedge formation.

34   Saxo says (*History of the Danes* VII.248-249, pp. 226-227) that Odin personally taught Harald the wedge formation; he also says that Hring's army formed, not a wedge, but a pincer formation, which is an effective defense against the wedge. Regardless, both Saxo and the *Sögubrot* make it clear that Harald's great tactical advantage has just been neutralized.

35   Saxo says that the battle lines extended all the way to Värmland, which would make them about 100 miles long.

36   According to Saxo, the last vile deed that Starkad must do will be to accept money to kill Ali in his bath under pretences of friendship, soon after this battle.

37   Saxi the Capable (*flettir*) is briefly mentioned in *Ynglinga saga* ch. 39 (trans. Hollander, *Heimskringla*, p. 42) as the foster-brother of Olaf Tree-Cutter, the son of Ingjald *illráða*.

38   An expression meaning "who has always won the victory".

39   In Saxo's *History*, Thorkel shoots Vebjorg with an arrow, instead of fighting her hand-to-hand. (VIII.262, p. 242)

40 An insult, but a correct one: according to *Gautreks saga* ch. 3 (trans. Pálsson and Edwards, *Seven Viking Romances*, pp. 145-146) and one version of *Hervarar saga* (trans. Tolkien, *Saga of King Heidrek*, pp. 66-67), Starkad the Old was the grandson of an eight-armed giant named Starkad Áludreng. Saxo reports a tale (which he himself doesn't believe) that Starkad the Old himself, not his grandfather, was of giantish ancestry and had six arms before Thor tore four of them off (*History of the Danes* VI.183, p. 170).

41 And yet, according to Saxo, he survives this battle. In *Gautreks saga* ch. 7 (*Seven Viking Romances*, trans. Pálsson and Edwards, p. 156), Odin had blessed Starkad with fame and victory in every battle, but Thor had countered by cursing him to be severely wounded in every battle. Saxo preserves other stories in which Starkad wins battles but suffers horrific wounds (*History of the Danes* VI.186, p. 173; VI.196-198, pp. 181-182).

42 Saxo says that Harald was riding a "scythed chariot"—presumably one with blades attached to the body or wheels—rather than holding the blades himself. He also claims that Harald was blind, although the *Sögubrot* states that Harald can see the battle. (VIII.263, pp. 242-243)

43 Saxo states that Bruni is driving Harald's chariot, and also makes it clear that Bruni is Odin in disguise. (VIII.263, p. 243) Neither of these facts is stated explicitly in the *Sögubrot*.

44 Saxo says that Harald was cremated, not buried, and that his ashes were taken back to Denmark for burial. (VIII.264, p. 243) Local legend has it that Harald's remains were buried at Lejre, the old royal center of Denmark, in a large mound now called *Hildetandshøje*, "Wartooth's Howe". However, the mound in question is now known to date from the Stone Age. (Niles, *Beowulf and Lejre*, pp. 280-282)

45 See note 20 above about the location of the earthly Alfheim, its two rivers, and its conflation with the mythical Alfheim.

46 *Skíringssal* (OE *Sciringesheal*) is mentioned in the Old English text of Ohthere's voyage as a trading town (Bately, ed. *The Old English Orosius*, I.i, pp. 13-16). Place-name evidence suggests that the archaeological site now called Kaupang, is the site of Skíringssal. The site may have been a royal center in the 700s; it once had a great hall and cemetery, in addition to workshops and traders' booths (Skre, "The *Sciringes healh* of Ohthere's Time", pp. 150-155). According to *Ynglinga saga* ch. 44 (trans. Hollander, *Heimskringla*, p. 46), the legendary King Halfdan Whiteleg is buried there; the saga makes him a rough contemporary of Sigurd Hring.

47 The present-day Oslofjord region.

List of Swedish Kings

1   *Hversu Nóregr byggðist* ch. 1 gives an account of Nor, his son Raum, and his grandson Alf, who is also called Finnalf (*Fornaldarsögur Norðurlanda* vol. 2, pp. 137-148). Alfheim, its rivers, and the beauty of its people are also described in chapters 6 and 10 of the *Sögubrot* (see *Sögubrot* notes 20 and 45). *Þorsteins saga Víkingssonar* also describes Alf the Old, Alfheim, and its rivers, but states that Alf was Raum's son-in-law (*Fornaldarsögur Norðurlanda* vol. 2, pp. 185-186).

2   This paragraph is in Danish in the original.

3   Probably to be identified with the present-day town of Ringshaug in the municipality of Tønsberg, on the western side of the Oslofjord, northeast of the Kaupang site.

4   This is of course Ívarr *viðfaðmi*, Ivar Wide-Grasp.

Tale of Ragnar's Sons

1   The word "morning-gift" usually refers to a gift given by a newly married man to his wife on the first morning of their marriage. It's not clear why the word is used here.

2   Literally "swore this oath at the *bragarfull.*" The *bragarfull*, "best of cups", was a ceremonial bowl or horn of ale or other drink. Oaths sworn over the *bragarfull* at feasts were particularly binding. The custom is described in the *Poetic Edda* (*Helgakviða Hjörvarðssonar*, trans. Hollander, p. 177) and *Heimskringla* (*Ynglinga saga* ch. 36, trans. Hollander, p. 39; *Hákonar saga góða* ch. 14, trans. Hollander, p. 107).

3   *Austrvegr*, "the east way", is the usual designation for the eastern Baltic.

4   In the Viking Age, Lake Mälaren was a navigable bay of the Baltic Sea.

5   Tulinius points out that this version of events, which is quite different from *Ragnars saga*, may derive from 13th-century Iceland, in which rival chieftains (*goðar*) might try to lure away each other's pledged followers (*þingmenn*). (*Matter of the North*, pp. 136-137).

6   Located immediately west of the Oslofjord, in southern Norway.

7   A mountain range in present-day Oppland, Norway.

8   The southernmost point on the Norwegian mainland.

9   The usual stereotype of the kings of England in the sagas is that they're friendly, kind, generous, not very warlike, and always glad of help from a strong and capable Norseman. Ælle is unusual in showing cruelty by executing Ragnar in the snake-pit. See Fjalldal, *Anglo-Saxon England*, pp. 101-112.

10 Like the story of how Ivar founded London in *Ragnars saga*, this story is not

true. York was founded by the Romans in the year 71, as *Eboracum* (probably "place of yew trees" in British Celtic), which the Anglo-Saxons turned into *Eoforwic* ("boar settlement"). The Vikings turned the name into *Jórvik* ("horse town") when they captured it.

11 The *Anglo-Saxon Chronicle* for the year 867 (trans. Whitelock, p. 45) implies that King Ælle was killed in the battle, rather than being captured and tortured.

12 Sighvatr Þórðarson was a skald to several kings in the 11th century. Eleven stanzas of his *Knútsdrápa* (*Praise-Poem for Knut*) have survived, including seven in *Óláfs saga helga*, chs. 145-149 (*Heimskringla*, trans. Hollander, pp. 435-441).

13 Roberta Frank ("Skaldic Poetry", pp. 170-172) has argued that all that the skaldic stanza really means is "Ivar killed Ælle and eagles scavenged his corpse"—a fairly common figure of Germanic poetic speech, in which eagles, along with wolves and ravens, are the corpse-devouring "beasts of battle". The gory "blood-eagle" rite may derive from a misunderstanding of skaldic figures of speech like this one; the expression "carved [i.e. torn and eaten] by an eagle" (*skorit ara*) could also be translated as "carved with an eagle." However, see Smyth ("The Effect of Scandinavian Raiders", pp. 17-20) for a peppery defense of the historicity of the "blood-eagle" rite.

14 No other source mentions Yngvar and Husto. The main source for King Edmund's martyrdom, Abbo of Fleury's *Life of St. Edmund* (in Sweet, *Anglo-Saxon Primer*, pp. 82-89) claim that Ingware and Hubba did the deed; Ingware is probably Ivar himself, and Hubba has the same name as Ubbi, whom Saxo lists as a bastard son of Ragnar. The *Þáttr* or its sources were presumably compiled at a time when it had been forgotten that Norse Ívarr and Anglo-Saxon Ingware were originally the same name.

15 King Eadmund of East Anglia, whose forces were defeated by the Great Heathen Army in 870. Now known in Christian churches as St. Edmund the Martyr. The *Anglo-Saxon Chronicle* (trans. Whitelock, p. 46) states only that he was killed during or after a battle. Abbo of Fleury's *Life of St. Edmund* claims that he was tied to a tree, shot full of arrows, and finally beheaded (quoted in Sweet, *Anglo-Saxon Primer*, pp. 83-85).

16 From this point to the end of Chapter 4, the text parallels *Óláfs saga Tryggvasonar in Mesta* (*The Longest Saga of Olaf Tryggvason*), chs. 63-64. Both probably derive from the *Skjöldunga saga*. (Guðnason, ed., *Danakonunga sögur*, pp. 84-90)

17 For more details of Bjorn Ironsides's raid on France, see Jones, *History of the Vikings*, pp. 215-218.

18 *Hervarar saga* (ch. 11; trans. Tolkien, *Saga of King Heidrek*, pp. 60-61) claims that Bjorn became the king of Sweden, and that his descendants included a king named Bjorn at the Mound (*Björn at haugi*). This Bjorn has been identified with

the king Bernus of Sweden that the missionary Ansgar met in the year 827 (Rimbert, *Vita Anskarii*, ch. 11, trans. Robinson, *Anskar*, p. 48), but this doesn't mesh well with other dates in the chronology.

19 The region around the Oslofjord.

20 The south coast of the Baltic, now part of Germany but inhabited by Wends (eastern Slavs) during the Viking Age and later.

21 The Danish historian Sven Aggesen claimed that "Sighwarth, the son of Regner Lothbrogh" killed the king of Denmark, assumed rule over the country, and married his unnamed daughter, fathering Knut. (*Short History* 4; trans. Christiansen, p. 55)

22 Not the same Horda-Knut as the one who held the throne of England from 1040 to 1042 (whose name is usually spelled Hardecanute in English histories). Sven Aggesen claims that a commoner named Ennignup ruled the kingdom while Knut was young (*Short History* 4; trans. Christiansen, p. 56). Ennignup may be the same as Chnuba, a ruler briefly mentioned by Adam of Bremen (*History* I.xlvii, trans. Tschan, p. 44)

23 Sven Aggesen inserts two generations between Knut and Gorm, making Gorm the son of Klakk-Harald. Aggesen calls Gorm *Løghæ*, "the Lazy", and claims that he did nothing but drink and enjoy himself. (*Short History* 4; Christiansen, trans., p. 56) *Jómsvíkinga saga* (ch. 1) says that in his youth he was called Gormr *heimski*, "Gorm the Stupid", although he came to be called "Gorm the Old" or "Gorm the Mighty" after reigning a long time. The *Historia Norwegiae* calls him "notably foolish" (trans. Kunin, p. 15). This may well be Christian propaganda; Saxo says that Gorm persecuted Christians and even tore down a church, "in order to restore the primitive worship to the shrines" (*History of the Danes* XI.318, p. 295). Adam of Bremen calls him Hardecanute Vurm, and claims that he was hostile to Christianity, while the *Ágrip of Sögu Danakonunga* calls him *harðr ok heiðinn*, "fierce and heathen" (Guðnason, ed., *Danakonunga sögur*, p. 327).

24 An inscription on one of the Jelling Stones calls Thyra **tanmarkaR but**, the runic spelling of *Danmarkarbót*, "Denmark's Benefit" or "Denmark's Improvement". Sven Aggesen (*Short History* 6-7, trans. Christiansen, pp. 56-61), Saxo (IX.319, p. 295), the *Historia Norwegiae* (trans. Kunin, p. 15), and *Jómsvíkinga saga* (ch. 2, trans. Hollander, p. 30) all praise her wisdom. Note that Saxo claims that Thyra was the daughter of the English king Æthelred.

25 Klakk-Harald, or Harald Klak, was one of several rival kings in Denmark in the 9th century; he allied with Louis the Pious and accepted baptism in 826, but was driven out of Denmark in 827 and settled in Frisia, holding territory there in fee from Louis. (Jones, *History of the Vikings*, pp. 105-106).

26 Adam of Bremen claims that Gorm was forced to submit to King Henry the Fowler, who blocked his expansion south of the Schlei; however, the chronology seems confused here (*History* I.lv-lvii; trans. Tschan, pp. 49-50).

27 According to *Jómsvíkinga saga* (ch. 4; trans. Hollander, p. 39), the English king who faced Knut and Harald's army was Æthelstan. Æthelstan died in 941, according to the *Anglo-Saxon Chronicle*.

28 Knut and Harald aren't mentioned specifically in the *Anglo-Saxon Chronicle*, but the *Chronicle* does mention Æthelstan leading the English forces to victory at the battle of Brunanburh in 937, near the end of his life. According to *Egils saga* (chs. 51-55), the opposing commander at Brunanburh was Olaf the Red, a descendant of Ragnar Lodbrók who ruled Dublin at the time.

29 Saxo states that Knut was killed in Ireland, although he agrees that Knut was shot from ambush while his men were competing in sports. (*History of the Danes* IX.321, pp. 296-297)

30 Harald was born around 935 and died in 985 or 986. For reasons that are unclear, he became known as Haraldr *bláteinn*, "Harald Blue-Tooth".

31 Arnulf of Carinthia, king of East Francia (887-899) and Holy Roman Emperor (896-899). In 891 he defeated a Viking force on the Dijle River, near Lovonnium (Louvain) in present-day Belgium, killing their kings Sigifridus and Gotafridus; the slain Vikings were so numerous that they blocked the river. (Jones, *History of the Vikings*, p. 226; *Annales Fuldenses*, pp. 119-121)

32 According to Snorri's *Edda* (Skáldskaparmál 64, trans. Faulkes, pp. 146-148) and *Hversu Nóregr byggðist* (ch. 2, in *Fornaldarsögur Norðurlanda* vol. 2, p. 142), Dag was a son of King Halfdan the Old, who sacrificed to the gods and was rewarded with the promise that all his descendants for three hundred years would be great men. Of Halfdan's eighteen sons, nine fell in battle; the other nine, including Dag, became ancestors of the noblest families. Dag's other sons are mentioned in *Hyndluljóð* 18 (*Poetic Edda*, trans. Hollander, p. 133) and in *Hversu Nóregr byggðist* ch. 2.

33 i.e. the raven has not avenged Sigurd Snake-in-the-Eye, the namesake of the famous hero Sigurd Fafnir's-Bane.

34 *nýtinjótar nás*, "fitting enjoyers of the corpse", is a rare kenning. Vigfússon and Powell (*Corpus Poeticum Boreale*, vol. 2, p. 352) translated it as "gentle winds" blowing on Sigurd's pyre. Hungerland interpreted the kenning as "ravens", so the line would mean something like "the ravens can whistle at him" ("Zeugnisse zu Volsungen– und Niflungensage", p. 135). Finnur Jónsson (*Den Norsk-Islandske Skjaldedigtning*, vol. B2, p. 261) rendered the line as "the ravens may now dispense with him". I've interpreted this kenning as meaning the flames of the pyre, consuming Sigurd's body.

35 From here to the end, the tale closely paraphrases Chapter 5 of *Hálfdanar saga svarta* in *Heimskringla*; the author may have copied this from *Heimskringla*, or perhaps both authors copied a common source. The "long saga of Sigurd Hart" is now lost.

Krákumál

1   The strait between present-day Sweden and the Danish island of Zealand.

2   The kenning Hedin's wife refers to the legendary endless battle between the kings Hedin and Hogni, as told in the *Sorla þáttr* (*Fornaldarsögur Norðurlanda* vol. 2, pp. 95-112). Hedin's wife Hild (whose name means "battle") resurrects all those killed each day.

3   In the eastern Baltic, according to Vigfusson and Powell (*Corpus Poeticum Boreale*, vol. 2, p. 342)

4   For more on the early medieval use of herrings as chopping tools, see *Monty Python and the Holy Grail*, scene 19.

5   Possibly Scarborough, England, although Smith argues against this possibility (*Scandinavian Kings*, p. 75).

6   Saxo refers to a location called Campus Laneus, "Wooly Field" (*History of the Danes* IX.303; trans. Fisher and Ellis-Davidson, p. 282), which is one way to translate *Ullarakr*. But Ullarakr could equally well mean "the field of Ullr", a god associated with winter and archery.

7   This explicitly Christian kenning suggests a late date for the composition of the poem as we have it, as do the kennings "Ægir's donkey" (stanza 18) and "string-notched palm-trees" (stanza 15) and certain other linguistic features. See Poole, *Viking Poems*, pp. 18-19.

8   Vigfusson suggests that this is present-day Hedinse, near Svold (*Corpus Poeticum Boreale*, vol. 2, p. 342). But the name may also have something to do with the legend of Hedin and Hogni; *Hjadningavágr* means "bay of the descendants of Hedin". See note 2 above.

9   Ole Worm mistranslated the Norse *varat*, "it was not", as Latin *erat*, "it was", and repeated the error in stanzas 14 and 18—accidentally implying that for the Vikings, fighting was equivalent to sexual pleasure. Thomas Percy and others who relied on Worm's translation perpetuated the error into the 19th century. (O'Donoghue, *Old Norse-Icelandic Literature*, pp. 114-115)

10 The identification of Vikaskeid is unknown; Smyth (*Scandinavian Kings*, p. 76) assumes that it lay on the east coast of Ireland.

11 Possibly the present-day Ålesund, Norway.

12 This kenning for drinking horns, *bjúgviðir hausa*, "bent trees of the skull", is

the one that was misinterpreted by Ole Worm and those who relied his Latin translation as "the skulls of our enemies", accidentally creating a now-stereotypical image of the bloodthirsty Viking.

13 *Dísir* are female spirits associated with a family line; here they are equivalent to the valkyrjur or valkyries.

INDEX

Æ

A

B

CPSIA information can be obtained
at www.ICGtesting.com
Printed in the USA
LVHW090829070719
623279LV00006B/201/P